## PRAISE FOR *OUR LIFE IN*

*Selected for the PRIX DU ROMAN FNAC*
*Selected for the PRIX LITTÉRAIRE DU MONDE*

'The reader will be captivated by Darrieussecq's hypnotic style.'
*Le Monde*

'The title could be "Our Life in the Future", but reducing
this book to a dystopian tale is doing it a disservice...A journal
from beyond the grave, as time runs out...And a profound
novel about loneliness.' *Libération*

'In this exceptional novel, the author of *Pig Tales* describes
a world in the future where surveillance is omnipresent
and clones rule...' *L'Observateur*

'Marie Darrieussecq is a writer of the body: the human and
animal body, the body in metamorphosis, the absent or foreign
body, the sexually aroused body, the grieving body...and now
android and robotic bodies...She returns to her favourite literary
subjects: the extremes of experience; that which is strange,
monstrous; the relation between creator and creation.' *Lire*

'Once again, Darrieussecq gives us a passionate investigation into
the deficiencies, transformations and lapses in our humanity...
A little like Ray Bradbury in *Fahrenheit 451*, she shows how
literature is our best means to disrupt functionality.' *Focus Vif*

'A disturbing dystopian tale in which tragedy and irony work
together...Ingeniously and brilliantly, Marie Darrieussecq's

sparkling tale adds to the classics of futuristic fiction. Even more profound than the social and political resonance of this novel is the theme of loneliness.' *Télérama*

'Reading Marie Darrieussecq is a true delight for the soul.'
*Ouest-France*

'In this brilliantly executed dystopia, Marie Darrieussecq writes with rare skill about the concerns of our time—the senseless destruction of the planet and transhumanist madness. Outstanding.' *Le Matin Dimanche*

'There is one surprise after another in this moving novel. In gripping, spellbinding prose, Marie Darrieussecq prepares the way into the future with passion and lucidity.'
*Madame Figaro*

'Who would have thought Marie Darrieussecq would write a thriller? This brief, feminist and political novel is perhaps her most inventive…With wit and elegance, the author takes us into a narrative full of tension, and with the same humour as in *Pig Tales*. Once again, she creates an absurd world, and denounces the failings of our society.' *Les Inrockuptibles*

## PRAISE FOR MARIE DARRIEUSSECQ

'Marie Darrieussecq reads the testament of Modersohn-Becker—the letters, the diaries, and above all the paintings—with a burning intelligence and a fierce hold on what it meant and means to be a woman and an artist.' J. M. Coetzee on *Being Here*

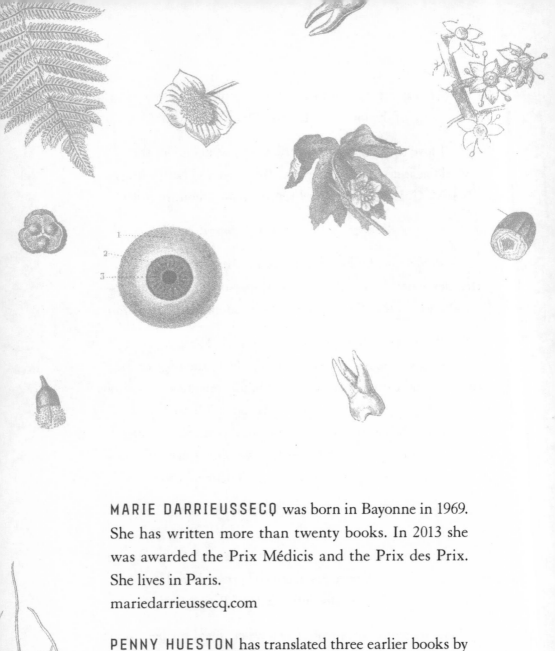

MARIE DARRIEUSSECQ was born in Bayonne in 1969.
She has written more than twenty books. In 2013 she
was awarded the Prix Médicis and the Prix des Prix.
She lives in Paris.
mariedarrieussecq.com

PENNY HUESTON has translated three earlier books by
Marie Darrieussecq—*All the Way, Men* and *Being Here:
The Life of Paula Modersohn-Becker.*

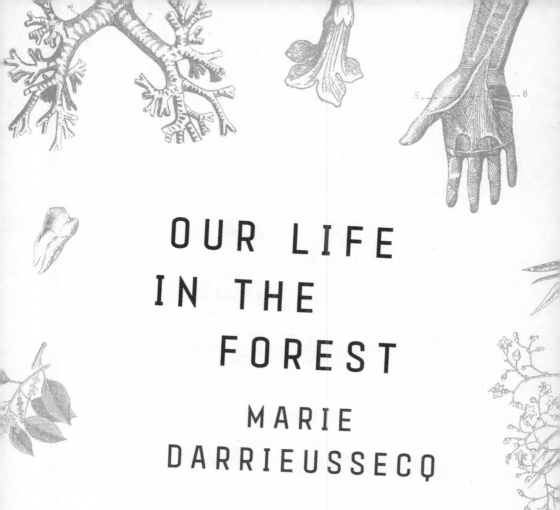

# OUR LIFE
# IN THE
# FOREST

## MARIE
## DARRIEUSSECQ

Translated from the French
by Penny Hueston

TEXT PUBLISHING MELBOURNE AUSTRALIA

textpublishing.com.au

The Text Publishing Company
Swann House
22 William Street
Melbourne Victoria 3000
Australia

Originally published in France as *Notre vie dans les forêts* by P.O.L Éditeur
in 2017.
This edition published by The Text Publishing Company in 2018.

Book design by Jessica Horrocks
Cover images by iStock
Typeset by J&M Typesetting

Printed in Australia by Griffin Press, an Accredited ISO AS/NZS
14001:2004 Environmental Management System printer

ISBN: 9781925603781 (paperback)
ISBN: 9781925626766 (ebook)

A catalogue record for this book is available from the National Library of
Australia

'I did not shoot the
wretched in the dungeons.'

Sergei Yesenin

I OPENED MY eye and *bang*, everything came into focus. It was clear. Almost all of us had our halves with us. And it was scary just how clingy my half was. A sissy. That's what I called her: Sissy. I had lost all notion of social graces. The only thing that worked with her was to push her around. A bit.

Time to get a grip. I have to tell this story. I have to try to understand it by laying things out in some sort of order. By rounding up the bits and pieces. Because it's not going well. It's not okay, right now, all that. Not okay at all.

She was immature, but that's normal. Considering the life she'd led. Considering the life she had to lead. Well, anyway. But I don't want to start in on my half. I'm sick of her. I could start with my patient, the clicker. Patient zero, in a way. I think it's thanks to him that I understand. He went mad, like a lot of people. Because of his work—at least, that's what he came for in the beginning. In the beginning, don't we all come for a reason that isn't the right one? I say that from experience.

First of all, let me describe my current situation—right now, because I've got a feeling I have to move fast. I don't have much time. I can feel it in my muscles, in my bones. In my remaining eye. I'm not in good shape. I won't have time to reread this. Or to write a plan. I'll just write it as it comes. So:

Around me I see an encampment in a forest. Tents and tarpaulins. Holes in the ground. Braziers. The canopy that protects us from the drones. A pirated internet set-up and a few DIY robots. Composting toilets and iron-fisted management. Back to basics.

The main advantage of halves is their flexibility. They can adapt to anything. Their biggest flaw is that they understand nothing. I had to teach mine everything. And I mean everything. Let me tell you: she didn't know how to walk. And that's just the beginning of it. Take a big, soft body, almost forty years old, even if she barely looks twenty-five, a gorgeous girl, and stand her upright, verticalise her: she opens her eyes, and then *bang*. She falls down. It's funny, that strapping young woman all of a sudden on the ground.

I learned how to verticalise during my internship with the babies. It works up to around four or five weeks. After that they've grown too much. You grab an infant by the head and buttocks: there it is lying in its cot, pretty well useless, and, hey presto, you verticalise it, put it upright just like you and me. Like the *Homo sapiens sapiens* that it is. And it opens its eyes. Magic. Even if it appeared to be fast asleep. It looks at you, looks around, contemplates its surroundings. It works every time.

It made us interns laugh, good, affectionate laughter. Anyway, verticalising my half—I was going to say my intern—was a big deal seeing that she's as tall as I am, 1.67 metres and half a centimetre, to be exact. I've always hung on to my extra half a centimetre. (To tell the truth, she's a good 1.68 metres tall: she hasn't been shrunk by life.) Well, anyway. So we worked it out with the other escapees. A few of us got together to verticalise our halves. We held their legs and shoulders by propping them up against a tree. I mean, what hadn't we already done to them anyway? Well, mine opened her eyes every time. Without fail. And she examined me. It was touching, but uncomfortable. Those blank eyes: dread, there's no other word. Where do you begin? I told her my name, Viviane, and then hers: Marie. My name's Marie too, obviously, but I'd chosen Viviane as my fugitive name. You have to comply.

Next came walking. Like a baby. It didn't take long; it was as if their mode of life had somehow instilled in them a certain amount of human data— first walking upright, then speech. The main thing was to beef them up, and to strengthen their tongues and jaws too; in short, to coach them in walking and in speaking. Orthopaedics and speech therapy was precisely what we were doing, in the forest. We worked on accentuating their human posture; we made them discover their voice. My professional training was useful.

Admittedly, we don't have much to do in the forest. Our activities are limited at the moment. It's a matter of fleeing in an organised fashion, but fleeing requires a lot of energy, believe me. We can't risk carrying the halves out on stretchers like we did in the beginning. There are too many of them now. They have to walk—fast. They had to learn to run.

They turned out to be useful for cooking, carrying water, digging tunnels and erecting tents, et cetera. Don't think I'm implying they're all women; there are men as well as women, of course, and even a majority of men.

Right. So where do I start? I don't think I have to explain the elementary precautions we're taking. They're obvious: the jamming of our digital data, of our identities, et cetera. The logistics of our disappearance. Our disappearance, the one they don't get to decide—that's what annoys them the most. We have all disappeared. Except that they know we're here, in a sort of reverse mirror of the world.

The planet is small. We discovered that pretty quickly. I mean, ever since the voyages of Christopher Columbus and Magellan and Cook and whoever else. (Columbus, Magellan and Cook were explorers.) And ever since we dived into the ocean depths, and onto the Moon and Mars, and Jupiter's satellites, and then the habitable planets, we no longer really have anywhere to hide on Earth. It's self-evident. And yet, oddly enough, we still manage it. It's extremely uncomfortable. You have to forgo what most domestic animals are entitled to: dry straw for shelter, accessible food, care and protection. If you accept having your feet constantly wet, and never again drinking coffee, and if you can forget about hot showers (I'm only mentioning the things I miss most), you'll manage to stay hidden. To disappear. As long as there are forests.

The logical thing would be for them to burn them all down. Or they could stockpile the wood from the native forests and plant huge fields of trees on a cleared forest floor, beneath a chequered canopy: no more undergrowth, no more gloomy light. It's on the drawing board. But I don't have time here to elaborate on ideas you already know, and which perhaps (one can only hope) you oppose. I am writing in order to understand, and to bear witness—in a notebook, obviously, with a graphite pencil (you can still find them). Nothing online about it. As lacking in technology as was the huge amount of manual energy expended at Lascaux or in the Sistine Chapel—well, I don't really want to compare myself to them. (Lascaux is a famous painted cave, and the other place is a famous church, also painted.) I bet my notebook will end up buried in a tin. Perhaps with me, before too long. My half will join me much later, in her own time. Of the two of us, Sissy will have the better life. The best life possible. Sometimes I say to myself that our ultimate aim in life, the most noble thing we can do, is to protect our halves.

I'm the elephant here. I've lasted a very long time. It doesn't happen often, but I'm going to end up in our cemetery, buried with the rites we established for ourselves. At least, I hope so. The vast majority of us die without understanding. Sometimes it goes to my head, the fact that I understand what's happening. Even if I don't understand everything.

Where were we? Time to get a grip. I'm cold. Patient zero, the clicker. Are you aware of what a clicker does? Their job is to teach the robots all our mental associations, so that one day they'll be able to make them instead of us. Which would allow them to work empathetically, et cetera. The clicker came to speak to me about the infinite tedium of his duties. It is envisaged that the project will be completed in about fifty years. But, until then, the job consists of staying seated in front of your device, and clicking every match between words and images, or words and sounds, or sounds and images, or colours and emotions, that sort of thing. You can even do it in your head if you agree to have your device implanted. You can do it while you're walking or under the shower, except it requires—as the clicker explained—complete focus. It seems like a mechanical process, but it demands concentration and speed. You're endlessly performing a task the mind can do but which discombobulates a robot. And which is nevertheless difficult to conceptualise. The only solution is to multiply the links, *click*, *click*, *click*, until the robot has been supplied with everything we could possibly have thought up until now, everything we could have felt, everything humanity could have experienced.

Blue = sky = melancholy = music = bruising = blue blood = nobility = beheading.

*Click*, *click*, *click*, *click*, *click*.

I think the last forest will have disappeared before the first robot is up to speed. We're nearly there. Fifty years. I won't be around for it. I'll have fallen to bits by then. I'm glad I didn't have a child.

So. The clicker. My clicker, if I can call him that, found himself stuck in a sort of cubicle where, all day long, he had to associate concepts like 'sadness', 'horror' or 'revulsion' with different types of attacks. Dismembered bodies, et cetera. Eventually, the images left him cold, but he didn't manage to get himself transferred to another job. He would have liked to work in the artistic section, for example—to associate Beethoven (a nineteenth-century composer) with 'beautiful' or 'musical', that sort of thing. But the clickers are controlled by somewhat rudimentary robots: it's a bit like when a shopping website suggests you buy shoes because you've just bought some, or go on a cruise because you wrote that you went somewhere by boat. Is the sight of blood always a bad thing? Is it always associated with horror? The clicker was asking himself these sorts of questions, all for a wage of two dollars an hour. Perhaps he was becoming subversive. Clickers get so bored that they spend their time chatting online; indeed, they unintentionally become real snitches. (Some of them do it intentionally.)

The first thing he asked me to do, when he came to see me, was to stay silent. That was a shock. This is not right, I said to myself. This one's going to cause trouble. I was trained to formulate a diagnosis, which is not that difficult, and then to steer people towards the most appropriate treatment—towards whatever will do them the least harm, as I say. But that's already expressing an opinion, it seems. I'm supposed to be perfectly neutral and benevolent. I manage to be benevolent because, for the most part, the patients are in my good books. If I sense something's not right, I refer them to my supervisor. (He's a strong-minded man; he even treats deviants.) Well, anyway, once I've made a diagnosis, such as hysteria with severe paranoid or obsessive tendencies (I have my own frame of reference, which I adapt according to the case), I listen to them talk for a bit, and then I direct them towards the various methods of treatment. But this particular patient, the clicker, did not want me to touch him, did not want me to speak to him, did not even want me to oversee his treatment. He wanted to ensconce himself in the armchair and, as he told me, rest.

'*Rest?*' I said. 'Do you have a death wish?' And he replied, 'For pity's sake, shut up.' So I latched onto the word *pity* and pointed out to him that death and pity were probably the concepts he would have to deal with most in his profession. But he told me he didn't want to talk about his profession—that it wasn't a profession, just a job, hard graft, his bread and butter, slave labour—and that if he could spend the half-hour granted by the occupational medical service, here, doing nothing, saying nothing, just resting and daydreaming, that would be fine, thank you very much.

Because of my diagnosis of 'depressed, suicidal tendencies, possible burnout', he was entitled to two sessions a week. Seeing him was also restful for me. Once I'd got used to the silence. His, but also my own. I have to say that I talk most of the time—perhaps too much. My supervisor says I prattle. The most effective treatment is Eye Movement Desensitisation and Reprocessing (EMDR), punctuated every thirty seconds by calming words. Inevitably, I was disturbed by this non-tactile and aphasic patient. My supervisor just said to wait and see. Literally. To be there, dependable. The main thing, said my supervisor, was that the patient knew he could come. The most important requirement of shrinks is that they are there. So that's what I did. The patient came, and he came back, and he ensconced himself in the armchair, and sometimes I wondered if he was asleep with his eyes open.

My supervisor was old; he'd been around for years and had made it into the new era, which meant he was experienced. Thanks to him, I put up with the anxiety of my patient's silence and immobility. I no longer even asked the question 'What are you thinking about?', to which the clicker would invariably reply, 'I think I'd do better to rest at my place than stay here', and I'd invariably reply that, actually, he did not know how to rest. And he'd ask me to shut up, for pity's sake. When I told my supervisor about the session, he also told me to shut up. So I complied.

I first met my supervisor when he was my own shrink. I was living a normal life: I worked, I took my dog for walks (I had a dog permit), I went to see Marie every fortnight. But no one could possibly think it was easy. Because of my circumstances, I'd been granted some free sessions with the shrink, two a week. I'd obtained visiting rights to Marie, thanks to my mother's persistence. And, all things considered, they'd observed that it did us more good than harm to visit our halves. There was even a period—you might remember it—when they advertised on the radio: in between advice to wash your hands and to drink when it's hot and to cover up when it's cold and to stay at home, those who belonged to the Generation were invited to make contact with the Rest Centres.

All of a sudden, I realise that's what they were called, Rest Centres; it just goes to show that it's useful to write things down, in order to clarify your ideas: *rest*, like my patient zero's favourite word.

Well, anyway. Rest Centres were where they kept the bodies. The bodies of our halves. It's still done, but I don't like to talk about it in the present tense. If I talk about it in the past tense, it feels like we've won. Where they kept the bodies…Back then, we didn't call them halves. I hadn't yet fallen in with anyone from the Generation, at least anyone involved with the Generation. Back then, I was going out with a guy called Romero.

Of course, I found it strange seeing Marie for the first time. How old was I? Fourteen? So I began a course of therapy. Two sessions a week to talk about Marie, and talk some more about Marie. Most people, all they do is talk about their parents. Or, if the worst comes to the worst, about their partner. About their children, their work, their lack of work.

And me: about that girl lying there. They've really messed us around. And that's being polite.

I didn't know I was pretty. At first, it was my narcissism talking. Honestly, I was fascinating. Then I figured out that Marie was much more beautiful than me. It wasn't exactly a mirror. She was the fascinating one, not me. I tried to get my head around the fact that she was not me. But it's not easy when you're faced with someone who sleeps the whole time. We would have had to converse. We would have had to meet. They use the word *meet*, but nothing happened. And yet there was a way of waking them up. Among visitors, we shared tips: speak into their ear firmly, not loudly, but with authority, an authoritative whisper. Their eyes opened. Their eyes opened briefly, as if in response to a large flashbulb. Their eyes opened so wide, huge and, let's be clear, terrified: we just had time to step back and stare into the large, panic-stricken whites of their eyes. Then their eyes closed again. And their faces sank back into their terrible serenity.

Marie is prettier than I am, I said to myself. That should have reassured me, actually. The psychologist from the Rest Centre disagreed with me. The psychologist said that we had the same nose to the millimetre, the same eyes, the same smile, the same jaw, everything, everything exactly identical, and so therefore I'm as pretty as Marie. But it's not true. Back then, Marie seemed to be forever immersed in a milk bath. Even today, her face is so smooth I want to murder her. She looks like the Mona Lisa. (The Mona Lisa is a famous painting from the sixteenth century.) When she was asleep, you'd have thought she was a horizontal Mona Lisa. Mysterious, contemplative. Thoughtful, my arse! Back then I didn't call her Sissy. That came later, when she had to be taught everything, and was frightened of everything, of the slightest scratch, of life in the forest. No, before we escaped, I called her Marie.

Don't count on me to structure all this coherently. I'm trying to follow a chronological thread, but it's not working. I should be telling it in order, but in my poor head it's like a leafy landscape with lots of valleys and alternative paths and people waiting, all half-dead, for me to let them speak, lickety-split. They're all speaking at the same time, and everything connects with everything else: the past with the present and with the future, what's happened with what's going to happen.

I'm cold. And my remaining eye is sore, and I keep trying to open my phantom eye. It feels like it's there, I'm aware of its presence under the scar, I'd just have to wink and all of a sudden it would open, and my phantom eye would allow me to see what I can't see.

My profession, the way I was trained, was to make the trauma people have experienced seem possible. I can't say it any other way. Even the word *trauma*—that needs to be discussed. By and large, terrible things have happened to all of us. More or less horrible, more or less sudden, more or less unexpected. For a human brain, the most difficult thing to understand, to accept, to *manage*, is the absence of any transition. For a robot, there's no problem at all; they're even programmed like that. But for a human being, a human being who is taking his child to school, who buys a croissant on the run and crosses the road with the little green man and waits among the parents and children for the school gate to open, without letting go of the little hand, and in the next second there's nothing but that hand in his

hand, the child's body having been obliterated—
I have a particular patient in mind—the brain quite
simply cannot deal with it. The before and the after
are not connected. They have no meaning. And,
regardless of all the stories one can tell oneself, they
never will. I was part of those teams of emergency
shrinks that were sent out after the big attacks at
the beginning of the millennium. A terrible time.
But I also treated run-of-the-mill accidents, the car
crash and the persistent noise in your head, the *bang*,
the ringing in your ears, the phobias that take hold,
routine trauma.

And then this clicker, who was referred to me
as a simple case of workplace stress. He'd been
involved in a skirmish; I wouldn't call it an attack.
When he was a kid in high school, they'd all been
locked inside while an assailant was walking around
with a machete. Some of my colleagues are treating
the assailants. I think I would have found that
interesting. Well, anyway, my patient managed by
himself to set things straight in his mind about
this incident, which had no more destroyed his life
than the day his mother announced to him that his
father was not his father—some things are routine

in the psychic life of human beings.

Go tell that to a robot. He'll give you his little concerned smile; he'll associate 'sad' with 'disturbing' but also with 'run-of-the-mill', if he's been well programmed. No, what tipped my patient over, and ended up preventing him from being productive, was quite simply the rhythm at work, of clicking fifteen hours a day in order barely to provide for his fundamental needs, and being in competition with Indians, Nigerians, Filipinos, Peruvians, all sorts of people who slave away as the planet's underclass and accept half as much pay as a white person. When I say *accept*, that word also needs to be discussed. Anyway. The masses of people in the planet's underclass who were prepared to go without sleep, that was what he found especially distressing. And the robots, of course, who never sleep. They know how to click and how endlessly to reproduce the most basic associations—love = happiness, passion = unhappiness—by grasping the difference between the passion for an idea, for a person or for, let's say, a sport or a hobby. The point was, robots don't sleep and my clicker really liked sleeping. He slept well. He was passionate about sleeping. Ha! He cut back when it came to food and living space, he didn't smoke, he almost never drank beer anymore, but if he was deprived of his sleep as well, he couldn't stand it. And he thought that was a perfectly healthy reaction. He needed, what was it, seven hours' sleep? But apparently that's a lot.

Sleep is for losers. It's what halves do. By this point in his treatment he'd agreed to talk, a little. As long as I shut up. I had no idea what to do, how to handle him, but I liked his vibe. When you're a shrink, you've either got it or you haven't: the feel for someone else's vibe. If you don't have it, find something else to do. A person's vibe. Like being in love. Enjoying it. Immersing yourself in it.

Sleep = rest = gentleness = bed = hibernation = anaesthetic = half = oblivion = death = anxiety.

In the beginning, as a young shrink, I often panicked, so I took notes. I filled in forms. The names of the grandfathers and grandmothers, paternal and maternal, places of birth, et cetera. The mother, the father. I checked the Register of Births, Deaths and Marriages, I read the CVs on my device. My elderly supervisor laughed. He was right: there's no point. It's all about the vibe. The patient shows up and everything comes back to you. Everything. By their presence alone—their gestures, their smell, the way they sit and look out the window or sigh and shut their eyes. The preceding two weeks or two years of therapy (even if these days no one stays for two years): it all comes back to you. In the absence of the patient it's erased or neutralised, but it's reactivated when the patient turns up. A whole universe. We used to call them unconscious memories.

After all, the unconscious does exist. That made my patient zero laugh. I only dared use the word once—the unconscious. I have no idea now what I was talking about. It must have been when he was telling me about his half, although I have no idea if we said 'half' back then. It's a kind of inappropriate word these days. How did we get on to this…He would go and see her—well, see *him*, given that his half was of course a man—perhaps once every six months, not very often. 'Still more often than I saw my mother!' he would say, laughing. He used to watch his half as he slept. It calmed him down. At least then he wasn't clicking. He was dozing. How many times have we, all of us, been woken up by the staff at the Centres? How many times have we, all of us, nodded off while we were watching our halves as they slept! He even thought about seeing it as a form of therapy, of using those rest periods as a way to avoid treatment. I pointed out to him that the classic arrangement—shrink in armchair, patient on couch, connotes the shrink as a mobile figure and the patient as a half. But he asked me, please, not to use the ridiculous word *mobile*. The halves probably just had to be woken up, he said, and then they'd be mobile like everyone else. (I wasn't so sure about that and the future proved me right: you have to teach them to walk.) Here we go again, he added: his brain was engulfed by the colour of the attacks. Once again he was seeing red.

Red = blood = colour = love = cheeks = wine = confusion = politics = anger.

How do you wake up the halves? Do they sleep from the moment they're born? Had they always been asleep? Or only during certain periods, like bears hibernating in the old days? Being permanently asleep is not good, I said to myself. It must harm them at some point. They all wore a nosepiece that released anaesthetic into them continuously. What happened if they were unplugged? Some said they would die. It was absolutely forbidden to touch them.

Where was I?

We are not allowed, either ethically or at all, to talk to a patient. Everything is recorded, of course, so there was no way we were going to muck around by stepping too far outside the framework of the treatment. I say 'too far' because this patient and I got talking a bit anyway. I liked him a lot (that's no reason). Back then, we thought no one, no one at all, would ever have time to listen to everything that was recorded every day in each room and each space in the human domain, or to view all those images. Those images, we said to ourselves, are made for after the fact, in case of a mishap, in order to identify victims and assailants. We didn't count on the watchful robotic eye and the robotic memory, or the endless time that machines have, their endless capacity for crosschecking. Whatever. I'm not going to tell you everything that happened afterwards, how we were all conned—you know it as well as I do. Let's get back to my patient. My patient and me. That could have been the title of this notebook, assuming it needs a title, but I don't want to talk about that at all. I want to talk about our life in the forest.

I want to testify that it is possible to be a nomad instead of being buried. Even if I'm cold.

'It suits you, your hair out,' he told me once.

I remember that. From then on, I never tied my hair up again.

He smiled at me and I smiled at him. He laughed and I laughed. He said to me, 'It suits you, laughing.' I didn't reply. I stayed silent. I remember that.

Where was I?

It's really difficult seeing out of one eye. It changes your view of things, and not in a good way. It diminishes the world: in particular, it flattens things out. I have a sore neck from trying to extend my vision on the left. It's as if I've lost half my head. Apparently, I always hold it at an angle. I am not aware of it, but the youngest among the halves make fun of me by imitating me: they walk hunched forwards like penguins (if penguins walked hunched forwards).

It's difficult lifting up a half. A half is at the same time submissive and insolent, a bit surly. Impertinent and sly. I'm not crazy about halves, but we've had to come to terms with them. After all, we weren't about to eliminate them.

'I did not shoot the wretches in the dungeons' is a line from the Russian revolutionary Sergei Yesenin, who is one of our Heroes. (There was a revolution in Russia at the beginning of the twentieth century.)

Of course we're armed. Our pirated robots are weapons.

Then again. Let me concentrate, with my poor eye. My patient. My patient zero. The clicker. I was supposed to give him a few sessions of cognitive remediation therapy. But he refused. That's not good, I told myself. How am I going to explain that? Remediation therapy works very well on traumatised people. You might say that my patient was not traumatised *enough*. I had to evaluate the effectiveness of the therapy every two weeks, then write up a report at the end of two months, four months or six months, depending on the length of the treatment.

I'll give you an example: one of my most resounding successes was when I treated the sole survivor of the Paris–Johannesburg flight shot down above the Sahara. You remember it. The woman buried herself in the sand because she had read somewhere that it would protect her from dehydration. She piled up all the bottles of water from the plane around her, all the meal trays, all the apples and even the ice-creams, melted and collected in a waterproof defibrillator satchel. She was surrounded, as far as the eye could see, by the tangled debris of bodies and metal, by seats to which corpses were still buckled, et cetera. She told me all about it. Yes, she was one who talked easily. Her husband and her two children had been obliterated; nothing of them was found, apart from a few objects. I'll spare you the list, but I remember each one of them: the soft toy and some other thingummy she kept mentioning in our sessions. I won't dwell on her subsequent phobia of planes—what could be more normal? And, given that she wasn't a flight attendant, we weren't about to go crazy trying to rehabilitate her to flying. You have to draw the line somewhere. The worst thing was that she could no longer manage to stand in a queue. She associated security checks—baggage, passports, body scanners, et cetera—with the accident. It drove her crazy, and I know what I'm on about. She could no longer wait anywhere. Not even to buy bread. Or go through any

25

sort of metal detector or inspection. And don't even mention a trip to the cinema. Or entering a department store. She could no longer do anything. Her life was in freefall. She couldn't even sleep anymore, because she felt herself falling.

Fortunately, her brain had erased the explosion. She had no memory of it. The fall, on the other hand, she remembered only too well. After all, it was ten thousand metres. This slip of a woman, thirty-five years old, falling ten thousand metres. There's time to change your view of the world. She had no memory of the landing. She is in the plane / she's falling / she's under the sand. That's the story. Before, she has a family; after, she doesn't have one anymore. Logically, she should not have survived. In short, a miracle woman. But, she told me, the whole time she was falling, nothing happened to her.

The syndrome of the sole survivor is well documented: the guilt, the feeling of being chosen, the mysticism, et cetera. Survival = relief = questioning = guilt = suicide. She didn't tick all the boxes. She had no mystical belief about being chosen, no relationship with God, no metaphysics, nothing. A down-to-earth woman. If I may say so. I can speak freely about her because she is dead and, as you will have understood, left no family. She committed suicide. That doesn't take anything away from the therapeutic method. Losing your husband and children just like that does not encourage anyone to stay alive. The therapy, even cognitive, cannot adapt people to everything—that was the conclusion of my report. I'm not afraid of calling a spade a spade. No miracle with the miracle survivor. I'm less comfortable with unexpected reactions, as in the case of my patient zero.

My miracle survior left me a letter that was easily authenticated. It's the only letter she left, given that she had no one apart from me—she had even stopped work. She'd become marginalised. There was no way out for her. Even so, without her letter, it would have been a close call for me, especially if she had gone ahead stupidly with non-assisted suicide. Non-assisted suicide is a nightmare for shrinks.

*Dear Marie,*
*Forgive me, you have done everything you could.*
*I can't sleep anymore, I can't eat anymore, even*
*breathing has become painful because it's the*

*same air as in my fall* [sic]. *I am writing this with a sound mind and am asking for my life to be terminated.*

Signed, et cetera, whatever the date was.

I can't get it out of my mind that it's a bit stupid to survive such an experience and then to ask to be finished off. Like when Primo Levi threw himself down the lift shaft. (Primo Levi was a twentieth-century writer, a survivor). Survivors have to learn from survivors. Even if nothing seems to compare to what they've survived. If you get what I'm saying. I haven't read that many books, but you get bored in the forest so you read what you can—printed books, of course. And quite a few of us write. There's a certain logic about us being under the trees with our old-fashioned notebooks and our old books, warped in the humidity, made from the same wood pulp that shelters us, and only able to be read during the day or under the light of the Moon. Not constantly connected to electricity, to the internet, or lit up all over the place. Oh, don't go thinking I'm old-fashioned. I have absolutely no nostalgia for the past, given that it has led to our present. I'm nostalgic for the future. Whatever.

Where was I? Oh yes, the therapeutic method. My miracle woman's suicide. Remission for her came with Eye Movement Desensitisation and Reprocessing. I was part of the only psychiatric unit not using drug therapy; instead we used three official therapeutic methods—verbal, ocular and cognitive. I had her recount the accident—it always made me a bit nervous when, right in the middle of a session, she challenged the meaning of the word *accident*; when she brought that up it was difficult to stop her—the *accident* as she had lived it, using the words she could find for it: horrific = appalling = speed = falling = cold = terror = life flashing before her = imminent death. And the death of her children and husband. Dreadful. She was alive but not living. And yet, the survival instinct. The hole she dug for herself in the sand. Like in a feature she had seen on Aboriginals. Opposite her, with my knitting needle, I interrupted her every two or three sentences and repeated her last words in a soft, soothing voice. I had her make eye movements in order to reprogram her brain. She followed the end of the needle (a sort of talisman I have from my mother; in fact it works

29

just as well with a finger or any light source). Rapid movements, always on the same side. Then you start again with another set of sentences and the same eye movements on the other side. At the beginning and at the end of each session she had to evaluate the level of her distress, from 1 to 10. It's a reassuring procedure. The level of distress lowers. The idea is to open a window of optimal tolerance to the highly charged emotions. And it works. Our brain is malleable. A lot more than the brain of a robot.

I was a good shrink. Reliable. I received glowing reports. My name was on the honour roll. Patient zero made fun of me. He's not the only reason for everything that came afterwards. But a trigger, for sure. The suicide of the miracle woman as well, I have to admit. I can still hear her murmuring: 'Falling is nothing compared to grief.' And also—she had this sweet, sad laugh—'Don't forget that what you call trauma is *unpleasant.*' Well, anyway. Later, I read studies that said EMDR is effective, but only in the medium term. She was found at the bottom of her apartment block; she'd thrown herself out the window, six months after our sessions. Is six months medium term? I still tell myself now, in the forest, that perhaps I contributed to an extra six months of life. Which is not nothing. And I was lucky enough to know her.

So, my patient zero. I called him that as a joke. He refused to be assessed in any way, no assessment of his mental distress whatsoever, nothing. But, since patients are required to fill in forms, he wrote zero on every one. Distress? Zero. Anxiety? Zero. The two of us ended up having a good chuckle about it, *cluck cluck*...My consulting room, the chicken coop.

He had two appointments with me each week. As he wouldn't have a bar of EMDR (Extreme Morbid Delirious Response was his version of the acronym—a lame joke), I used reprogramming methods that were more classic, perhaps more acceptable. Resistance to treatment is a phenomenon that Freud identified early on—I'm not going into it. (Freud was a psychiatrist around 1900.) I asked him to imagine a *safe place*. Safe-Place Therapy.

At first, as he didn't trust me (that's normal), he came up with the most clichéd places possible. Because of his clicking, he was an expert in clichés: island = paradise = coconut palms = white sand = heat = turquoise sea. I pointed out to him: 1) that a safe place has to be a familiar spot, not a screensaver;

2) that these days this type of safe place was engulfed by tsunamis, et cetera. He liked my objections a lot. 'I recognise a rebel when I see one,' he shot back. He would not normally have said something like that, of course, but it was a response taken from a mainstream film, and robots recognise stock phrases and isolate them as sound bites. Their vigilance is not faultless. Anyway. The clicker finally coughed up a safe place, some sort of clearing. A clearing from his childhood. He was born in the country, in a bit of remaining countryside. There was a wooded reserve below his house. In this reserve, there were enough trees to form a clearing. As a little boy, he thought it was a real clearing, like in fairy tales: a wall of trees around a circle of fairies. He felt good in this clearing. It seemed to him that nothing could harm him. He was surrounded by airwaves and all that, but at least he couldn't see any houses or roads, or schools; his father and mother were faraway; only the occasional aeroplane or drone passed overhead. There were still a few insects, firebugs mostly, some caterpillars and a few earthworms, a butterfly from time to time. So, yes, he was willing to imagine the clearing as a safe place. Indeed, it did him good.

And, to tell the truth, before my encouragement, he was already imagining the clearing whenever he felt bad. I simply suggested he use this remedy more systematically.

He kept on at me about it: 'An *imaginary* safe place? It's not bomb-proof, your safe place. It would not withstand, for example'—he lowered his voice—'torture.'

'Neurologically, our brain does not distinguish at all between the imaginary and the real,' I replied. 'You can tell from the recordings. We get negative and positive emotions mixed up; we associate badly because of our trauma. If you are frightened of spiders, for example, it doesn't mean that you were already attacked by a swarm of spiders: that's an imaginary fear!'

'But I'm not frightened of spiders,' said my patient patiently.

My supervisor was right. I talked too much. I prattled.

'Oh, but you're frightened of everything,' I said to him. 'Why did you come to see me? Because you're frightened to *live*.'

And I pointed to the two charts on the wall,

33

one taken from the classic Alcoholics Anonymous Treatment Program:

*Give me the serenity to accept the things I cannot change.*
*The courage to change the things I can change.*
*And the wisdom to know the difference.*

The other was from the principles of good management:

*Luck is only an excuse to abdicate responsibility. I know that I create my own reality through my way of handling events and of interpreting circumstances. I focus on the solution rather than the problem, on the action rather than the reaction, on opening up rather than withdrawing.*

I used to say to patients, 'Be yourself! Come as you are! Get a grip!'

'Know what you want, who you are and why you are here!'

Now that I'm in the forest, I wonder who I was when I was thinking all that.

I'm cold.

With my patient zero I began to understand myself. I mean, to understand what I was saying.

34

I spoke less and less. And he spoke more and more. It averaged out. I think we spent half the time not saying anything. Which makes for a lot of silence, especially when it's being recorded. Even if only robots listen to it.

I mean, when I grasped even just a fraction of what had been done to me, I often used the safe-place technique myself. When my suspicions became unbearable. I'm not even talking about the chronic pain, the breathlessness, the dizziness, my eye…no, I'm talking about the idea itself of what was done to us. Of the *concept*. And, in practical terms, the team that was mobilised to do it. The actions they carried out. The decisions they took. That's when I imagined myself in my safe place.

My safe place was already a forest. So it's not surprising that the clicker and I got on well. I think it defined us as human animals. The forest. The trees. Most patients imagine an interior place: a room in a house, a kitchen, their childhood bedroom or, conversely, a huge, light-filled hall. For exteriors, they come up with meadows covered in flowers, lakes, or actual caves. I had one woman whose safe place was a cave *under the sea*—best not to

35

be claustrophobic. But the forest is traditionally a rather disturbing place. I think so. Remember fairy tales like 'Hansel and Gretel'. And the myth of the wolf. The wolf is among us, now, today. In the city, in the zone, and in almost all the safe places. I'm talking metaphorically. If you get my drift. I don't know where the real wolves are anymore. Back when Tsar Whoever-it-was built St Petersburg, people refused to go and live in the far-flung estates. Not so much because they were far from the city centre, but because they were near the wolves. The Neva froze, or something or other, and the wolves invaded the city. I can just imagine the tenant explaining to the real-estate agent that it's really nice, as a neighbourhood, but that, even so, there're a few too many wolves. That you could never be sure you'd arrive home in one piece. Ha!

Anyway. My safe place. I visualised a forest. I'm not about to pour out my damn childhood. For God's sake. Let's spare ourselves that. But I visualised a forest that I went to as a child. It lay just beyond my grandparents' garden. In a vanished world.

But I had a parasite leeching off me. My half. Marie. I couldn't pretend Marie didn't exist. Even if in my childhood I hadn't yet met her in the flesh, or seen a photo of her, so what. Marie was with me in the forest. I mean, she was inside my head. Usually they call that an imaginary friend. Imaginary, my arse. Marie was perfectly real. A sister I'd never seen, asleep, constantly monitored, like a penned animal, but whose existence I have always been aware of. The proposal made to my parents was not the sort of proposal they could refuse.

The moral of the story: very soon after my own birth, a surrogate mother gave birth to Marie, who has exactly the same genetic material as me, and who has always been presented as a life insurance policy, for me as much as my parents, since we all came from the same stock. A long-lasting body. If one of us needed a new organ, the transplants would be perfectly compatible. Marie = a supply of spare parts. The half = a safeguard. Anyway, that's the way they spun it for us. And, for pity's sake, I'm not about to dish up the same platitudes for you.

On his patient information form my patient zero had ticked the box 'holder of an earthenware jar', as did a lot of the upper-middle-class. Whereas he'd told me that he had a half. But he wouldn't talk, wouldn't be assessed, nothing. Only spoke when he wanted to. He referred to a jar metaphorically, as 'a potty'. 'Sit on the potty.' It made him laugh. Apparently metaphors produce bugs in robots. He also said that, if you want to disrupt a robot, you have to overuse double negatives. Along the lines of: 'You're not going to make me not believe that you have not understood that I am not a non-being.' In any case, he was fascinated by stories about halves.

'Look at you,' he used to say. 'You're always coughing. You're taking such deep breaths,' he'd say.

And after my kidney transplant. 'You're as yellow as a low-wattage light bulb.'

Sometimes when I was with him, I felt as if I was suffocating. I'd open the door and he'd come in and my heart would start pounding. My poor heart.

My missing eye—that's what took the cake. And of course he was cunning and never gave me any *geographical* clue as to where his safe place was. He was like the butterflies that are dying out. My patient is the first person whose disappearance I have tested. I mean, I actually witnessed his disappearance, what we call a disappearance: chosen, wished for, organised by the missing person.

He taught me what duration is. Let me explain: normally patients turn up and I choose between the three therapeutic methods. I get started and they get started and off we go. But he didn't want any of the three methods. He didn't want *anything* to happen. Half an hour is a long time. Sitting opposite each other. Not necessarily looking at each other, but doing nothing. Letting time pass.

It doesn't seem like a big deal, but I still wondered whether I should be asking him questions or something. I held off. He looked out the window. Both he and I had been assigned accommodation without windows. My consulting room, on the other hand, was a pleasant place, thanks to this opening. You could see the reddish clouds and, twenty-five storeys below, a corner of the city. If you leaned out you could glimpse the real ground beneath the walkways, the little shops run by the illegal immigrants, the puddles of water. He told me that he used to walk there sometimes, on the real ground. You could make sense of things there.

Most of the time, I looked at him. I've never got to know a face better, apart from Marie's. I would have recognised him anywhere, even with my eye problem. Anywhere, anytime. I sighed. He looked at me. He smiled at me mysteriously. (It's easy to look mysterious when you don't say anything.) Then he looked out the window again. Time passed like in a clepsydra. I think that's the word for a water clock. Like water that falls in little beads, *plop*, *plop*. Or that rolls like a little drum, *brrum*, *brrum*. You could hear our rustling, the sound of the fabrics we were wearing, the saliva on our lips, the creaking armchairs, the footsteps in the corridor. You could hear the noise of time.

'That's all splendid!' my supervisor said.

Supposedly this patient was finally turning me into a *psychoanalyst*. (My supervisor was at least eighty years old.)

I've also been trained as a sexologist. That's the fun part. I'll tell you about it another time.

During my final sessions with the clicker, I talked about myself. About my anxiety over my eye. He asked me if I was certain that my illness was serious enough to justify such an operation. He said the fact that he'd had to miss out on sessions because of my so-called chronic illnesses had really got on his nerves during the whole course of treatment, and that it wasn't normal for a shrink to let her body lead her around by the nose, and that it was as plain as the nose on my face what was happening to me, losing an eye on top of everything else. We used lots of metaphors when we chatted, despite the robots. Robots' comprehension is literal and metaphors disrupt their crosschecking: they must have been saying to themselves that we were obsessed by our noses. Nasophiles, ha! They're hopeless at double meanings and they have no sense of humour. Especially with spoken language, robots confuse raise and raze, sent and scent, lyre and liar, pair and pear, sole and soul, cunt and can't...Even I didn't properly understand the weird things the clicker said. That, in the country of the blind, one-eyed people ruled. 'You've got a bit of robot in you too,' he told me. 'You need to grease your wheels a bit.' I coughed and he quoted Molière (a writer from the seventeenth century who died of pulmonary tuberculosis) at me: 'Your lungs, your lungs!' Ha!

One day, he didn't turn up.

The consulting room was completely silent. I heard a different sort of silence, an emptiness, dust motes flitting in the air, disturbed only by my weak breath, and the heat of the red sun at the window. He was no longer there. His armchair was empty.

I stayed sitting opposite the armchair for the duration of the session. I contemplated his absence. He was somewhere. I could have sworn he was alive somewhere. Of course, I can't write his name, or describe what he looked like, his size, his mannerisms, what he smelled like, his voice, the little wrinkles around his eyes. The inflection of his voice, never nasty, when he made fun of me. 'Irony condemns, cynicism sanctions.' It's one of his sayings that has stayed with me.

My patient, the clicker. What a damn nerd he was. One among millions and millions of clickers. The last human job for the masses in the whole world. Shrinks, for example, are still needed, but not many of them. Compassionate robots are doing better and better. Why, in the forest, am I thinking so much about my old job? It's like I'm missing it— the listening, doing what I could according to the limitations of my methods. Well, there you go.

He'd been there, twice a week, and he wasn't there anymore. Nothing, no early warning sign, not a word. He was something else.

It didn't have the same effect on me when my miracle patient didn't turn up. Her absence, I mean. Of course, I'd already received her letter, which confirmed her suicide and asked if I could please forgive her. Well, anyway. She also talked a lot about the halves. Even so, we're not supposed to treat people just because they have halves. Technically, in fact, it was her husband who had a half: he was from the Generation. She only had a jar, a basic jar—heart/lungs. You're lucky if you have a half. To be able to transplant bits and pieces, et cetera. To be able to patch yourself up all over, not just your heart and lungs. But I think at that time (it was before my patient zero), I was not at all comfortable with the idea. Not that one is ever comfortable with this idea, perhaps. Whatever, I didn't have a clue about anything at all. My supervisor was also encouraging me to talk about Marie. I told him that coming from the Generation had a number of advantages, in terms of employment, housing, career and of course life insurance, seeing that we were all constantly ill or sickly. A lot of researchers and doctors used us as case studies. Our condition was psychosomatic: our bodies manifested the mental stress we were apparently enduring. Ha!

That's not good, I used to say to myself, when my miracle patient got on her hobby horse, the halves. It's only going to exacerbate her trauma, twist the knife in the wound without providing any sort of clue about her timeline. And what's more, it's going to get us both into trouble. A half is absolutely no use at all in the case of total destruction of a body. But she was obsessed with the idea of returning to the desert in order to double-check the spot. The corpses. She wanted the bodies. Of her husband and of her children. It drove her mad—and let me tell you, I know what I'm talking about. 'Do you think it's normal,' she said, 'that my husband's half is alive, and he's dead?' (Her children only had jars. Anyway, just try getting jars to come back to life.) 'Do you think that's normal?' she asked me. And yet she knew that we are not our halves. She knew perfectly well that the thing fast asleep was not and could never be her husband, José. A tragic likeness. And yet she couldn't help going to see him. Holding his hand in the Rest Centre. Talking to him, to her husband's half. It was too much for her. I didn't manage to revive the process of compatibility between her and her timeline. She committed suicide.

Adjustment = progress = improvement = balance = overcoming = satisfaction = wellbeing = success = freedom.

All of that happened before my patient zero, but it still upset me. I reported it to my supervisor, but I was struck with more and more frequent feelings of suffocation. I was born with only one lung. Thanks to genetics, Marie naturally had two—she's perfect—so I underwent a pretty serious operation, at the age of three, in which they transplanted one of Marie's lungs. I have no memory of it, but my mother often talked about it; she cried every time and that upset me. The transplant never really took properly. The scar was painful. The skin tissue is so stiff, I can scarcely raise my arm. And I'm always short of breath. The shrinks treating me at the time used to say my anxiety was compromising the success of the transplant.

The very fact of Marie's existence caused me a lot of distress as a child. Even though she was just a sort of sleeping sister. A twin, almost. And, for my mother, an extra daughter. A reliable stand-by.

Anyway. I had trouble breathing. From early on, I was treated for asthma. I developed a bit of a complex about the scar. Left anterior thoracotomy. My breast grew—well, both breasts—over the scar, and I hoped they'd grow large enough to hide it. But no. When I was fifteen I understood that I'd be a B cup forever. With a big, bulging red mark under my left breast.

I had trouble stripping off. Afterwards things just got worse.

And, what's more, that lung of Marie's bothered me. I saw so many shrinks, it's not surprising I became a shrink myself. I don't know, perhaps I imagined I had a debt to repay. But not as much as my debt to Marie. Her real name, if I can say that, was a long sequence of numbers, imprinted in my memory but which I still have trouble writing down. I made a request to see her. To see 269017510200880-Thingamajig. Whatever. I remember the forms that had to be filled in, delivered one morning before I left for school. I carted them around in my damn schoolbag all day long. I couldn't understand why it wasn't happening in the normal way—virtually. They were real papers, hard copy. To fill in by hand. The drone came back: there were documents missing. I attached them, with the help of my mother. The drone came back again. It went on like this for weeks. This is not good, I said to myself. And then finally, ha! I got the clearance. A delivery guy came and implanted an ID tag, *pop*. It sat under the skin on my wrist; I beeped at the gate of the Rest Centre every two weeks. That's how it began.

We're not allowed to touch them. We're not allowed to touch our halves. I had no idea how to deal with this proscription.

I had taken her lung. Her left lung. It bothered me.

The shrinks did their utmost to get me to draw my timeline, but apparently my timeline integration went badly. My timeline only had fifteen squares, given that I was only fifteen years old. The first four were reconstituted memories, since I couldn't remember anything before the age of four (which is pretty late, so it seems). Anyway. You've all inte-grated or at least tried to integrate your timelines, so you know the deal. I chose one memory per year, and did one drawing per square. For year fourteen,

I drew a drone, to represent the long administrative procedure to get the clearance to see Marie. For year thirteen, I drew a sanitary pad with blood on it, because getting my period was a big deal for me, whether you like it or not. For year twelve, I drew the whole class, all the students one by one, leaving a big empty space for my friend Mathias Matéo, who disappeared. For years eleven, ten, nine et cetera, I'll spare you the details. For year three, I drew a lung. The one I took from Marie. Bright red. Like cat-food animal lungs. The shrinks were not pleased. In their opinion, it meant a lot of blood on my time-line. For them blood = danger = fear = disgust = wound = attack = death (perhaps they were robots). Too much blood. In short, they were asking me to choose between my breathing and my period. Between my uterus and my lungs. They suggested I draw something more positive, like a dandelion whose seeds you blow away. A dandelion? To represent reproduction? No, for breath, air, wind. But I had never seen a dandelion, except in pictures. And, anyway, I think in a timeline you should draw things you've seen for real, that you've experienced with your own senses. Correct?

Well, anyway. For year two, I drew a man, who looked like what I imagine my father looked like, dead, killed by his toaster (I drew the toaster as well). For year one, I drew myself and Marie. I drew *us*. Year zero: our birth in the same year. I drew two women, with big bellies, my mother and another mother, holding hands. I drew my mother wearing the checked raincoat she always wore.

Here I am telling you my whole damn childhood.

The shrinks told me I'd done a bad job integrating my timeline: it was too grim. Admittedly, my life had not been without tragic events. So they told me. But has it not come to that for all of us? (I remember that sentence, its slightly odd syntax: *But has it not come to that for all of us?*) Did I really care about connecting my birth with Marie's? We were *not* twins. Twins, identical or not, share the same uterus. Apparently, when you come to draw your half, it's normal to depict it as smaller than yourself. In my drawing, Marie and I are exactly the same size, which is the absolute truth. (Marie, as I mentioned, is even slightly taller than I am. Sort of longer—from lying down for so long.)

For year sixteen, I didn't draw the death of my

49

mother. It was too painful. I drew a dog. The shrinks thought that was good.

Where was I?

You couldn't tell from looking at Marie's face if she was in pain or not. I would have liked to lift up one of her arms to see if it caused her pain, because my lung had been removed from her. But don't even think about lifting up an arm. It's forbidden to touch the halves. They're *hooked up* in every which way, fed intravenously, et cetera. She was breathing peacefully. She didn't look unsettled. The halves breathe through a little nasal tube. Which dispenses, continuously, what used to be called laughing gas (ha!): enhanced nitrous oxide. It's also an anaesthetic, so I learned: hence the absence of any signs of suffering in her features?

So. The first time I saw her. My mother was not allowed to come with me. She died soon afterwards; she joined the father I never knew. She had the same sort of stupid domestic accident. An electrical mishap. The subsequent devastating events meant that a lot of housing and electrical installations were declared illegal. The fact remains that I was left alone at the age of sixteen. Nothing unusual there.

The shrinks steered me towards their own training. There was a strict quota for shrinks, but they could always help me find a job.

A terrible time.

I got my dog licence. I called my dog Wolf. Let's be clear: it was not a wolf-dog. I think they're reserved for the police. He was a good dog, a whippet, a little greyhound. Super-fast. Wolf. His name was in honour of the wolves of St Petersburg, who terrorised people, preventing them from living peacefully in their new residential estates. On his record card his name was Docile. Really, what sort of a name is that? 'Docile, heel!' Anyway, I never said 'Heel' to my dog. I hate clichéd expressions. And any sort of orders. It's something I've come to realise in the forest.

They delivered the dog to me when my mother died. It's a form of orphan benefit. Supportive relationships are the key to neuronal integration. Obviously, orphans have a harder time of it. The shrinks used a certain number of compassionate strategies. There are a lot of orphans, so they have to breed up a lot of dogs. Very occasionally cats, but cats are less supportive.

He was a real dog. A modified dog, of course, but a real dog. A real non-human animal. I signed for the delivery quickly and read the record card while the drone deposited the dog. He had been given a tranquilliser injection for the trip. He also had an implant in order to adapt to life in an apartment, the type of windowless studio I lived in. The implant neutralised a range of urges, like sex and running. Docile. Docile, my arse. I can say it here: I removed his implant. I could feel it rolling under my fingertips, in the fold of skin under his ear. I pulled the skin hard—the dog was compliant, of course—and gave a *snip* with the scissors. We have all become surgeons in this world.

In the forest, our dogs run. They run fast. What joy!

Later, I found a dog, not born in the breeding factory or anything. I didn't give him a name. What gives us the right to name them? We are neither their parents nor, technically, their creators. All the dogs in the pack that travels with us now are called Dog, and we assume they consider us as a group of human animals, each recognisable by our olfactory trace.

During my first year with Marie, I wished I could take her to the zoo. A completely unrealistic wish, of course, but I couldn't suppress it. I mean, I even dreamed about it at night. When I was little, my mother sometimes took me to the zoo, and then she no longer had the time. The main attraction at this zoo were the mammoths. They have managed to recreate several couples elsewhere on the planet: I think there's a pair in the Leipzig Zoo, another in China perhaps, and then ours. There were also dodos, which look like huge turkeys, and a Tasmanian tiger. Several bears, a group of penguins, a whale in a huge aquarium and all sorts of extinct animals. But the mammoths were something else. I wanted to see them again, and show them to Marie. It was a stupid idea, obviously—she had never even seen a dog, or a pigeon, for God's sake.

Mammoths are a magnificent sight. A mammoth's body is one long slope, the body rising towards the head. The head is enormous, as are the tusks. It's as if the enormous neck is a buttress for the edifice of the head. They walk slowly; swinging in front is their immense curved ivory scaffolding, which looks as if it's been handcrafted. I'd never seen anything like it. A mammoth's coat is a chestnut colour, almost orange, and very thick. Their little eyes look at you as if they've known all about you forever. A memory like a mammoth's. And that languid calm. In the next enclosure there was the little herd of female Asian elephants from the breeding factory, their surrogate mothers.

The Tasmanian tiger always made me sad because he was alone. And restless, nothing calm about him at all. He would roam around his enclosure, around and around. He ended up excavating a deep tunnel along the fire fence; you could watch his twitchy striped back pass by in front of you. The rest of his body disappeared below ground level.

In the forest, I've come to understand that zoos are museums of extinction. And that the whale, although fully whale, had something artificial about it. Firstly, despite the efforts of the humans, the aquarium was too small. A whale is not exactly designed to swim laps. And also, even if it was supposed to be the *same* whale each time, at whatever age I was, five, eight or eleven, I knew that they replaced the whale on a regular basis. She'd been called Willy for ever and ever, and they were always re-cloning her, because whale clones are very unstable and have a lifespan of only a few months in an aquarium. That made me sad too. Such an enormous load of fish sold at high prices to fish fanciers. Don't forget that the fish sales paid for the breeding, processing and handling of the next whale. Needless to say, this form of systematic animal harvesting, condemned by some, obviously doesn't encourage the development of research on non-human animals—I mean on their life expectancy, their sustainability. The cloning of non-human animals is nothing more than slaughter—that's what I've been told in the forest. Anyway, my dog Wolf has been alive for six years.

So. Suffice it to say, I never took Marie to the zoo. And I understood very quickly that Marie could not be taken anywhere. Technically, she was not untransportable, but in fact there was no way at all of carrying her. And, anyway, it was already such a business getting there, to the Rest Centre—I was going to say to the zoo—getting myself there.

In the beginning, my mother requested time off and took me. She didn't want me making the long trip all by myself. First we caught a tram, then we got off at ground level and went by communal taxi to the north gate. They let taxis through, even taxis packed like sardines. There were always mechanical bugs in those old automatic taxis; sometimes they wouldn't let you out at the right spot.

As we approached the edge of the city, the sky became redder and redder. The last stop was already in the zone, then a stretch of countryside with empty sheds and abandoned rubbish tips. After that we had a long walk along a disused train line to the entrance of the grounds where the Centre was located. So, the trip took us more than three hours, one way. All the Centres are set in remote places out on the fringes of the city. And my mother was only allowed up to the gate with me.

In the beginning, rain, hail or shine, she would wait for me, sitting wherever she could. She would start knitting or turn on her low-tech reality device, slip on her headset and try, as she told me, to *detach herself from the situation*. After all, Marie was her child too, in a way (even if later I learned that not one bit of my mother's genetic material was in Marie).

I would head across the grounds, glancing back

at my mother as I walked. That's how I see her in my mind now. I don't know why the image that comes to mind when I think of her—you know, when I think of her without thinking about her, when she *comes to mind*—is this woman sitting on the ground against a high gate, huddled inside a checked raincoat, hunched over but craning towards the virtual images, her face forward, half-hidden by her headset. A tortoise.

After a few visits the tortoise started to object—always when I was going through the identity check. It was embarrassing. She put on a whole performance in front of the robot cameras, as if that was going to achieve anything, insisting that she too wanted to go inside and demanding to see her *other daughter*, and what the hell were they breeding inside? 'She's *my* daughter!' she screamed, and I was at a loss to know whether she was talking about Marie or me. 'It's *her* body!' yelled the poor woman. Eventually, they dealt with the situation, the increasing number of visitors, by building a small shelter for the support people, with heaters, benches, a coffee machine and state-of-the-art speakers transmitting augmented reality. They constructed the shelter exactly where my mother used to sit. But she was already dead by then.

There's this African tale—the tortoise who flies with the birds. The tortoise is presumptuous enough to fly, and then for some reason the spell breaks, and the tortoise falls from the sky and is crushed to death on the ground. Since that day the shell of a tortoise has looked like the pieces of a puzzle stuck back together.

Where was I?

I've seen tortoises in terrariums. Sometimes you can also see one in the forest, wild or released back into the wild. I like to imagine it's my mother.

It approaches very slowly and I give it some grass to nibble. I keep the dogs at a distance. I'm wearing my mother's old checked raincoat and leaning against a trunk. During the whole time it takes for the tortoise to come closer, I'm thinking, trying to remember that person who always called herself—with such kindness, and such passion—my mother.

Let's get back to it. We followed the old train tracks on foot and my mother sat down in front of the gate and I had my ID check and I went in.

I don't know if I was shocked the first time I saw Marie. In fact, I find it difficult to remember. The first time has become part of the other times. They all merge together. So much for chronology.

I saw this extremely pale face, which had never seen the sun. Eyelids closed, the eyelashes casting a shadow, like several rows of eyelashes beneath closed eyes. A beautiful fringe of eyelashes. Perfectly still eyebrows, a smooth forehead, cheeks without a single flaw. And the sheet under her neck. Not exactly a sheet but a sort of space blanket, shiny, pearly white. A material better suited for their protection, apparently. They're very sensitive to skin irritations. Their exposed arms, covered by a white garment, the same for girls and boys, with puffy sleeves, fitted down to the last nanometre. Like a bubble of fabric around them—which we removed as soon as the halves arrived in the forest. And the hands, especially the hands. Bare. We weren't allowed to touch them. But once we'd managed to get permission, it was for the hands.

We were allowed to rub cream on their hands. That's what you do to people in a coma.

I feel like I should be focusing on the first time, on the meeting, as it were, on my first memory of her. Or my first contact with her. But nothing comes to mind. Quite simply, I think I was stunned.

So I massaged her hands and nothing happened, no expression at all on her face. Not even a quickening of her breath or a change on the encephalogram— which was not a flat reading, no, just very regular.

I'm telling you the specifics of all this because people are always talking such nonsense about the halves.

All the other treatment to do with cleanliness, excretion, et cetera, and especially muscular exercise and the prevention of pressure sores—all that was carried out by a specialist team, without us, outside visiting hours. They also shaved the halves' heads. I should have begun with that: there was the resemblance, of course, what we called the mirror effect, but, in particular, there were those shaved heads. For hygiene or whatever. It was weird. On top of everything else. I would have really liked to do her hair.

I knew the whole business of massaging their hands served no purpose, beyond the initial satisfaction of the physical contact. We knew the halves weren't dead. They weren't mannequins or anything. Their skin was warm and soft and normal and, as is the case for all of us, their breath contained vapour. Anyway. So I preferred simply to hold her hand. And I stayed there a long time, sitting on the folding chair next to her bed.

Honestly, when my mother died it was a weight off my shoulders. Don't go thinking I'm a monster. What I mean is that, from then on, I could stay for as long as I wanted, for the whole visiting time, without worrying about my poor mother, left behind, sitting outside, her back against the gate, craning forward over her low-tech virtual world, the rain or blazing sun beating down on her.

I knew the way by heart: tram, communal taxi, then walk along the train tracks after the zone. I didn't care at all if it took me one hour or three, or if it was a bit dangerous, because I had the whole day to myself. For me and Marie, whom I contemplated in her sleep.

As a result of holding her hand, things happened that I wouldn't have noticed if I hadn't stayed there all that time.

We were never technically alone with our halves. I forgot to state the obvious: there was always a nurse with us, male or female. They were robots.

Humans tend to fall asleep in this type of situation. Robots never get bored.

The male or female nurse stood tirelessly at the foot of the bed, with Marie and me in his or her field of vision. That was how the monitoring system worked.

'Don't you want to massage her hands?' the male or female nurse would ask. I answered no, because if you said nothing, you'd have this bunch of robots on your back the whole time. He or she gave a stupid little smile. And, fifteen minutes later, the same question, or a variation on it. Did I want a glass of water? *Trit trot*, off to the drinking fountain, *trit trot,* back with the glass of water. I wanted to smash them in the face. Those big bastards, ratting on us. You're not drinking your glass of water? Yakety-yak.

I tried to concentrate on the minuscule variations between her hand and my hand. I spoke to her. I told her the tale about the tortoise, for example. I also spoke to her about my mother—our mother, I should say. I tried to describe my mother in neutral terms. I don't know if such a thing is possible. I didn't want any trouble. I laughed to myself as I recounted her crazy habits, how she used to imitate bird songs in the morning to compensate for their absence, and how terrible it was (I imitated her imitating them), how she unplugged all the appliances for a few minutes a day 'to have some peace'. Peace, my arse! (Anyway the appliances killed her—she was electrocuted.) I would have liked Marie to laugh with me. For her to laugh, full stop. At me miming my mother. I must have looked like a lunatic jumping up and down by myself on my folding chair.

You never knew when the doctors were going to do their rounds. I think they were human beings, but perhaps they were new-generation robots. They moved so quietly in the dormitory that we used to joke they were on ball bearings. They had a kind word for each one of us. I don't know what they called that place but we called it the dormitory. I was one of the first visitors to the dormitory, presumably thanks to my mother, who was always kicking up a fuss, and who had spent so much time and energy on procuring the forms and helping me to fill them in, et cetera. And after a while there were ten of us visiting at the same time. The dormitory was huge: an old guardroom in a chateau that had been converted into a private hospital. There were old fireplaces, closed off to prevent draughts. Everything was painted white, even the fireplaces, with a plastic waterproof coating that looked like a plaster cast, like a space that was completely washable (which it was). It smelled like disinfectant and flowers; I mean, I think it was floral-scented disinfectant. Our halves gave off no odour at all, or very little—just the handcream (which they supplied). It was absolutely forbidden to bring anything into the Centre. We had to go through sensors, et cetera. And when there were almost as many visitors as halves, we were actually queuing. Back then, we were all between the ages of fifteen and twenty-five.

I tried to think of what to say to her. Honestly, I racked my brain. I got to the point of telling her about the films I used to see on Sundays. The doctors told me that Marie didn't have the slightest idea what the cinema was. Fair enough, since according to them her brain is empty. 102008-Thingamajig-Whatever is a non-person, they kept telling me. A bundle of organs. Contingency provisions and life insurance. That's that. I don't know why, but I saw her as the future. A blank page to write on. So much possibility. Raw material, in a way. Afterwards, a lot of us developed Pygmalion syndrome.

(Pygmalion was a mythical Greek sculptor.)

I'd see dreams gliding beneath her eyelids. She dreamed like cats: her eyeballs moved and her fingers twitched slightly, as if she wanted to scratch something. What was she dreaming about? About lying there? About sleeping? About the rustling of the sheet? Or about her birth, possibly her only waking experience? About a purely organic experience, moist and red, internal, about the beating of her heart, about the expansion of her lungs? (Of her *single* lung.) Sometimes I'd wonder about the limbo she was held in; perhaps it was not some sort of white material but rather a black abyss, in which she was chased by hunters. A stifling universe, where she saw organs throbbing, decomposing or ready to swallow her. I woke up with a start. I was having Marie's nightmares.

For God's sake, even asleep, how do you live through the fact that, one by one, your organs are being removed? Wouldn't you somehow be aware of it, dimly?

As soon as I'm sick, hey presto, they fix me up with one of Marie's organs.

The doctors told me that what I thought were

her dreams were nothing but a nervous twitch in her eyelids, a tic brought on by immobility. After all, they explained, our eyes are not programmed to stay permanently shut. No doubt 102008-Thingamajig-Whatever's eyelids wanted to open from time to time to exercise the muscles; to exercise *the capacity for opening*, as one of the doctors explained—a surgeon, to be precise. 'When it's possible, it has to happen,' he explained. 'We restrict the movement in 102008-Thingamajig-Whatever's eyes, her legs, et cetera, but they have to be seen as springs that want nothing more than to be activated.' I think that was his clumsy way of justifying their scientific method: what is possible inevitably occurs. He had no idea (perhaps he was a robot) that I was distressed by what he was telling me.

The shrinks told me that it was quite likely my half could dream. That even a dormant brain reacts to stimuli. That the mere touch of a hand, or the sheets, or the faint noises from the corridor, would probably be enough to produce primitive dreams in these chronic sleepers. After all, a dream is nothing more than a neuro-electrical discharge that produces random images gathered during the day by the unsleeping person. Constant sleepers collect this material however they can. In us, the sequencing of these mental discharges seems to produce stories, whose incoherence should alert us to their random nature. According to the shrinks, the superstition attached to the interpretation of dreams no longer has a place in our day and age.

But Marie's dreams spoke to me. I dreamed them. They were dark, motionless voids. This is not good, I said to myself.

Marie's fate became the most important thing in my life. I pretended to be passionate about my studies (indeed, when I started work I really liked looking after my patients). But Marie was constantly in the back of my mind. Not in the back: she was the permanent screensaver of my thoughts. She was there, dozing in my brain. I visualised her in my grey matter; she took on the shape of the lobes of my cerebral cortex; she was implanted in the spirals, curled up. I talked to her all the time. I was connected to her all the time. Even with her, I prattled. When I was moving my knitting needle into a patient's field of vision, introducing soothing words every thirty seconds—your phantom pains will disappear, no one is stalking you, everything will be all right, you will become accustomed to the absence of your arm—I had to unplug this sort of mental current directed towards Marie. Sometimes I thought that my words alone, communicated to her by some kind of telepathy, were keeping her...if not awake, then at least not dead in her limbo.

The doctors never failed to remind me that I was breathing with one of her lungs. And, later, that I was filtering what I drank with one of her kidneys. And then there was talk of my taking one of her eyes, when I suffered serious trouble with my vision. Surely, I said to myself, this type of physical relationship is bound to create a bond.

With the explosion in the number of visitors, the doctors started calling us by our names and avoided referring to the halves by their numbers. It was something I noticed. Nicknames were encouraged, like Pépette or Momo. Those two were right next to Marie in the dormitory. 'How's Pépette going today?' the doctors asked my neighbour. It was a way of asking her how she was, given that there was never any problem with the halves, despite the organ removals—which proved that they were a good thing. If you never move and never expend any energy, you can live for a very long time. You never wear out. Ha! Sustainable bodies. Sustainable bodies, my arse.

It was Momo's awake half who came up with this thing of speaking to them, right into the ear, in an authoritative voice. Momo's awake half was Moses, one of the very few black people in the Centre. I forgot to talk about that.* I've also barely mentioned the male–female discrepancy: there are approximately a third more men than women. It's something my girlfriends without halves, who only have jars, or *nothing*, call luck: 'You're lucky to be able to meet so many guys.' In Psych, I have to say, the students are mostly female. Anyway. Luck, my ovaries. That's not at all my thing. I did, however, try to glean as

---

* I also forgot to say, or I've barely touched on it, so I'll quickly add a footnote—that'll teach me not to write an outline—that we didn't really have much of a clue about what to call ourselves. I mean, us, the visitors to the Centre, the awake ones, the mobile ones. 'The awake halves' sounds nice enough, but when we nodded off at their bedside, holding their hand or whatever, the only difference between them and us was the chair and the bed: one collapsed on the chair, the other lying down in her white cloud.

much information as I could from the male visitors. There was no available information about the halves, only rumours, fake info, nonsense. The training we received at the Centre, in order to be granted regular visiting rights, was mostly about individual adaptation, the anatomy of the organ removals and that sort of thing, as well as the fact that their brains were empty.

Speaking into their ears in authoritative voices, but still in a whisper. Well, anyway. We had to wait until the doctors left the dormitory, pretend to cuddle our halves, without touching them, just resting our heads on the pillows and whispering. Trying to look sentimental, melodramatic, whatever we felt like. Increasingly, concepts like 'melancholy' or 'nostalgia' were associated with the word *half*—it was the robots' way of getting a grasp on things. Those decent clickers organising the world into intelligible categories. Half = incompleteness = likeness = emotional attachment pathology = nostalgia = compassion = depression. Well, anyway. We whispered, we sang lullabies (as if the halves needed to fall asleep!), and then, all of a sudden, we said, 'Wake up!' Or variations along the lines of: 'Aren't you sick of sleeping the whole time, you layabout?' Or even: 'Get up, you fat slut!', depending on our mood. We had fits of laughter. The robots on standby snapped to it, but for them hysterical laughter = adolescence = innocence, so it was all okay. And the half would open her eyes. Both eyes. At once. An awful, anxious, terrified look on her face. That moon-shaped face. It looked like it was all about to happen: they were going to push themselves onto their elbows and stand up.

But it only lasted a second. Their eyes closed again. Their dumb faces sank back into the depths of their expressionless masks. They really didn't look that much like us. They all looked like each other.

I developed a disorder called prosopagnosia. I could no longer recognise faces. I could no longer even discern the objective similarity between Marie and me, between Momo and Moses, between Pépette and Juliette. But it was especially bad outside: I got faces mixed up. The doctors and nurses all looked alike, and, once I walked out of the Centre, and was in the communal taxi and the tram, it was all déjà vu: every new face looked familiar. Once I was back in my neighbourhood, worn out from the long trip and the day at the Centre, even the people I knew, the baker, or my old neighbour in the upstairs apartment, seemed—in a disturbing, not reassuring way—to have a definite degree of family resemblance. And the worst was that I didn't recognise my mother in photos, not in 3D or even 4D.

The shrinks explained to me that déjà vu is a neural condition. The exhaustion of all those trips. You should have a rest. You're developing a morbid attachment—we're seeing it more and more in the Generation. Consider déjà vu as a form of augmented reality: when you see an ordinary thing, a face, recognisable or not, or any landscape, it's endowed with a certain cognitive coefficient—on seeing whatever it is, you supplement the fact that you think you've already seen it. It occurs in whichever lobe of the brain, a defective synapse that connects memory and vision. The brain thinks it remembers, whereas it's only seeing. Memory becomes a parasite on perception.

Holy mackerel! They made me sit a whole lot of tests. Nothing to report. My condition settled down. And then, months later, it actually got a whole lot worse. When it came to facial recognition, I was confusing vertical and horizontal lines. Morbid prosopagnosia. I contracted a serious degenerative disease in one of my eyes. They're considering a new transplant in the not-too-distant future.

I have green eyes, quite an unusual green that verges on turquoise, with a golden halo around the pupil. I really like my eyes.

I don't mind telling you that the news was very unwelcome. And to think Marie would be disfigured, one-eyed, thanks to me. But her eyes are useless, the doctors told me. Not long before, they had enrolled us all in a 'self-reboosting' training course, to improve our self-esteem: it wasn't our fault if we were afflicted with nasty illnesses. It was due to air pollution, the coal we were sent by retrograde countries that still used it for heating, chemicals in food, genetically modified organisms everywhere. We got sick. There was nothing we could do about it. That's what the halves were there for.

I put off the surgery for as long as possible. Anyway, I could still see well enough. They weren't about to teach me how to see. I'm the one who does the seeing, not them, I told myself.

Well, anyway. One of my dormitory neighbours, Romero, was in the bed opposite—that's how I got to know him. He only came to the Centre two or three times. Afterwards, he was the one who contacted me to ask if we could see each other again; I hadn't even thought about him. But he was good-looking and he was always explaining stuff to me, and he was perhaps the only person I have ever met who talked more than I do.

He didn't fall for the halves in the slightest. He told me that the halves would never wake up because they were not programmed to; they were *unable* to do so. He went further than the doctors: the halves were merely receptacles for organs, *our* organs; that is to say, from the start they were nothing more than waste material. At least we pay tribute to corpses; we bury them and cry over them. They are bodies that contained *people*. But the halves were already only dismembered bodies: a jigsaw of detachable organs, in abeyance. Hence the reasoning behind the jars: the vital organs are cultivated and maintained for their own sake, without the confusion of a humanoid likeness. Our so-called halves, he explained, are jars in our own image, neither more nor less. Sophisticated sarcophagi that are really just containers.

Romero was brilliant. He hadn't developed any sort of morbid attachment for his half, for his *proto-jar*, as he called it. He had never tried to wake up his half. 'What's the point?' he would say. Perhaps it was sport that helped him adopt such a detached position. He was super-sporty. In fact, in addition to his job, he competed in pentathlons. For those who don't know, modern pentathlons involve cross-country running, horse-riding, swimming, fencing and shooting. The complete athlete. An extremely expensive sport, but the country was at the forefront in this area—horses in perfect condition were made available for the athletes, along with pistols (loaded with blanks, of course) and buttoned fencing foils.* And of course swimming pools and athletic stadiums.

Romero's body was spectacular. In perfect proportion, lithe and strong, like a Greek god's. And his face, too, was completely different from that of his beanpole of a half. Tanned from all the outdoor

---

* For the sake of caution, I can't tell the whole story here. You should simply be aware that these two items were used as offensive weapons—thanks to me, I'm telling it like it was—in our grand escape plan for the halves.

sport and fresh air, toned to perfection, even his jaw, the cheeks chiselled from his physical exertion. A red-blooded man. Romero was a guy with a strong will. He used to say, 'I am the complete man.' I understand why he couldn't identify with that thing lying there.

Romero was lucky: he'd never fallen ill. They had never interfered with his half. He didn't have any scars on him. That's also perhaps what I found attractive about him: his extraordinary good health, as well as his total absence of guilt, and for good reason. I could picture the body of his intact half. Under the hypoallergenic material of his isolation bubble. Pallid and soft, of course, but with no incisions. Never scarred. When I pictured Marie's body, under her various layers of space blankets, I projected onto her my own scars: the bulging one under my breast, and the one on my lower back, on the right side. I saw it when I twisted in front of the mirror at home: it was also red and raised. The two spots where her organs had been transplanted. What did her body look like? Was there a hole under the sewn-up skin? Did they make an effort to give her aesthetically pleasing scars?

Romero was smooth and strong. Hardly ever available because of his training, but when we saw each other it was good.

Where was I?

Oh yes. The walk along the train tracks. That long walk to go and see Marie—let's not call it a stroll—did me good. When it comes to the shrinks' talk of pathological attachment, I wonder if I wasn't addicted to walking. To the movement of my legs and also to the unfolding of the landscape.

It was a wooded landscape. There are, of course, a few trees in the city, mostly plane trees and pines, but no forest, obviously, not even a grove of trees. The very last scheduled stop for the communal taxis was the paper plant. They still make paper for women's sanitary pads and that sort of thing. As soon as I caught sight of the paper plant, I had to walk for a long time with the stink of pulp in the air, and then it dissipated once the train tracks entered the forest. Of course, the wire fencing along the tracks prevented me from going into the forest, but all the walking meant I had time to feel detached from the city. I don't know how to say it: my rational thoughts remained back there, in the city, disintegrating as the journey continued. The rhythm of my walking allowed me to concentrate simultaneously on Marie and on the trees, as if the two things went well together. People don't walk very often anymore, and in any case never on the actual ground. I let myself be carried along, my head in the trees and my heart with Marie. Sorry to be sentimental.

I had no idea about the names of the trees, but they looked real. I mean, they hadn't been planted simply for fodder or wood. The huge fields of trees along the train tracks gave way to a forest like the ones in fairy tales: it looked wild and rampant, but was in fact tiered, small trees beneath big trees and ferns further underneath. I listened out for birdcalls or animals—one can always dream. But I never saw any on those trips.

And then I reached the grounds of the Centre. The metal gate opened onto a little sealed road, which must have been for private-vehicle access only. The trees here looked even more ancient, towering and huge. And then the chateau appeared in the distance, scarcely more than a country house, if you want my opinion. It had once been a five-star hotel, and a sanatorium, and before that a real chateau,

I believe. And then I'd swipe my ID under the robot cameras at the gate, et cetera.

At the mammoths' zoo, I also had the chance to see a lot of trees, extinct trees. Mahogany and ebony, the black poplar and the Easter Island toromiro tree and the western red cedar from Sichuan and the Basque oak. I took notes. I like plants a lot. We don't think enough about what a tree is. Indeed, the root of the word *clone* is the Greek word κλών, which means 'twig'. (I didn't read that on my device— we've banned them—but in an old etymological dictionary that I cart around with me from camp to camp. I'm doing research. It helps me.)

Anyway. Where was I? The trip, along the train tracks, the walk, alone. But once visiting restrictions were eased, I hardly ever had the opportunity to walk the distance by myself. They ended up organising communal taxis that went up to the chateau and back to the gate.

During years eighteen and nineteen of my time-line, I observed the almost exponential growth of the movement to reunify the halves. I think the word *half* became truly widespread, even popularised at that time. *Re-u-nite all our halves!* That was the slogan in those days. As if joining the pairs was going to redeem the whole Generation. And then things went from bad to worse. Everything shut down. There was a new wave of attacks, et cetera. We were frightened in the tram, in taxis; we were frightened at school and in the shopping centres; nobody went into the street anymore and never, ever anywhere directly on the ground. We hardly ever went to the Centre. I would say that, as of year twenty of my timeline, I must have only gone there twice a year at most. And there was Marie, who didn't change a bit, I mean she didn't age. At thirty, you'd have thought she was twelve, if it weren't for the two bulges under the sheet, her breasts. In fact, even today she has the mental age of twelve, Miss Sissy.

And a lot of people disappeared. It was the period of huge waves of kidnappings. The waves crashed down on us. The news service broadcast a sort of weather forecast of the tides of kidnapping and the deluges of disappearances and the floods of attacks. It was a time of disruption, which left us feeling helpless, and perhaps guilty, because if you get yourself kidnapped—through being foolhardy, too daring, outspoken—it lands your employer and the whole community in hot water. It leaves a hole in the social fabric. It was always made very clear to us that there would be no ransom payment, and there never could be. During the waves of kidnapping, we stayed home as much as possible. Protected behind our miserable seawalls. Locked away behind our piers. (They're metaphors.) We even stopped getting deliveries: the delivery guys frightened us, especially the drones. But it's difficult, in fact impossible, to stockpile food in our extremely small living quarters. I slept on sacks of rice and lentils. I felt safe in my bed. It was an illusion, of course, but in my bed I could take time to summon up my safe place. I wandered around in my forest from a long time ago. I tried to remember moments from a long time ago, in the forest beyond my grandparents' house, swampy and full of frogs. Well, we heard them singing. (I don't know if you say 'singing' for frogs.)

What's more, the lift had broken down. Permanently broken down. The robot repairers no longer came to my neighbourhood, and the lift robot itself no longer talked to us. Dead. Kaput. My very old neighbour upstairs was quite simply dying of hunger, incapable of facing the twelve flights of stairs. I already thought I was going to drop dead from asthma myself. A few of us got together to do her shopping. Nice neighbours, good sorts, like me. I had a soft spot for that old neighbour. She kept plants on her landing—she nurtured them from cuttings year after year, real plants that grew towards the light filtering through the roof. She was lucky (sort of) to live on the top floor; even though there are leaks, you get the fanlight. In our type of neighbourhood, the downstairs floors are dark. Anyway, we made arrangements: she got money out of her wardrobe and gave us enough to buy her potatoes, bread, half a litre of milk. An apple every now and again. Another neighbour managed the roster on his device and sent us notifications. It was easy. And then that neighbour got into trouble because they told him we were an *association*. He should have asked for a *permit*. Come on! So we made the arrangements verbally, as it were, by passing notes to each other under our doors. All right, written arrangements, if you like. Without using our devices. And then, dammit, another resident found the old woman lying dead in a pool of blood, her wardrobe open and her pittance gone. A terrible time. We even had to have a whip-around to pay for her cremation! The plants died. I tried to look after some of them at my place under a lamp, but actually it's true: plants can't survive without sunlight.

I'm cold.

It was around this time that, as well as my eye issues, I was diagnosed with a renal problem. I didn't want any talk of a new transplant, but after a month of nonstop dialysis at the hospital I resigned myself to it. I had the operation. I have no memory of it, which is normal, what with all the anaesthetics. And they say it's better not to remember. I can't say they're wrong. After treating lots and lots of traumatised cases, with only moderate success in the medium term, I'm convinced in the end that it's better not to remember. Bad memories are like toxic organ grafts, difficult to uproot; at best they can be fenced off so you can't go and graze on them. Bad memories = weeds. Best not to have them at all, or to invent good memories for yourself instead, so you can reprogram your brain. So you can *plant a new garden.*

I was in pain during the post-operative fog of my kidney transplant. I thought, here we go, I know all about chronic pain, here comes more of the same to plague me. I went along with having an electrical box implanted. I'm sure some of you have them too. It's an electro-neuronal device that sends little corrective charges into the neural circuits. Not so different from the implants we've all already got. It calmed me down. Get a grip, I told myself. And obviously I had new medications to help the kidney transplant to take. Even though the kidney was Marie's flesh and blood, and therefore identical to my flesh and blood, I still had to take a pile of medications. The electrical box apparently reduced the amount, as well as the side-effects.

Anyway. The pain has almost completely disappeared. And the transplant wasn't rejected. They just told me to drink a lot of water. But it contributed to my break-up with Romero. It wasn't the pain or the transplant or anything. It was the electrical box. One unfortunate remark from him. 'Look at you,' he said, 'a robot like the others!' He didn't mean that everyone is a robot. No. He meant that, despite my training as a shrink and my three therapeutic methods for curing trauma, and the way I prattled on the whole time, I caved in like everyone else.

As they say, I abandoned my principles. I agreed to be hybridised. Something like that. To tell you the truth, I don't even know anymore why I reacted so violently to his remark.

A terrible time.

On top of that, Romero didn't like dogs. He refused to have Wolf at his place. Wolf, my dog, my supportive relationship. Romero thought that, whether they were robots or not, dogs were a disappointment. I understand that you could get annoyed at seeing a dog robot, even a perfect imitation, always doing the same tricks with his ball and always placing his head in the same affectionate and clichéd way on your knee. I understand that. Robotics has a hard time reproducing the unexpected side of dogs. But Wolf was a real dog. Modified, of course, but a real, biological dog. Romero had already had a dog permit, and a real dog, which had lived for two years. But he didn't get another one. He used to joke that in two years the dog never learned to speak. You put a lot into a dog, he said: you walk it, you feed it, you look after it, you teach it to be clean and to heel—but that's it. It will never learn more than that. It will never become human.

He was joking, for sure, but something about the whole thing bothered him. Like a lot of us, Romero had lost his parents at a young age—I don't know whether one thing explains the other. He used to say that, at two, his dog was probably a lot stupider than a newborn baby. We argued about the word *stupid*. And we wondered: were our halves stupider than dogs? We tried to make sense of it all as best we could.

Romero was whole apart from his teeth. It took me a while to realise. We hardly ever spent the night together. I mean, I never slept at his place because he got up so early to train. One evening, however, there was something or other, an attack or a blackout, and a lockdown, so I was stuck at his place. What with the noises from the street and the fact of not being in my normal environment, I couldn't sleep; my whole memory of that night has been reduced to the sight of Romero's dentures in a glass of effervescent liquid. A row of teeth mounted on a pink base that resembled gums. All his lower teeth were false. He slept peacefully beside me, in a sportsman's restorative slumber, deep and sound. I resisted the urge to push apart his lips like you do on a horse. To see. His bottom lip did in fact shrink into his mouth with every breath. It wasn't very sexy. Above all, I wondered what was going on with his half? Did his half have the same depression under his lip? Why hadn't they transplanted the half's bottom teeth onto Romero?

'Are you going to stay like that?' I asked him in the morning. 'Aren't they going to give you a teeth transplant?' As if it was the first time his body had been violated (and it probably was, but this time it was horribly visible), he got angry: it didn't diminish him in any way; I was not supposed to see it; he'd have the transplant after the Olympic Games, blah, blah, blah, otherwise he wouldn't be fit enough. On and on.

The whole nation pinned their hopes, big time, on Romero in the pentathlon. And when he lost, wiped out in the heats, he died a few days later from a heart attack. He had just requested, at my insistence, to be scheduled for a teeth transplant.

It's too bad about teeth. They're too conspicuous. But still, less so than hands. I don't know if you noticed that those of the Generation who have to undergo hand grafts disappear pretty quickly after the amputation—well, I knew of a case. A post-operative complication. Eyes are risky too. And the heart too, obviously—invisible but deadly. Ha!

Romero and I split up immediately after that incident. I mean, after our argument. I really liked making love with him but I think that, at the time, I wasn't capable of truly loving at all. Of loving a person. They call it attachment disorder. Attachment disorder, my arse.

I told you I was a sexologist: one of my special areas along with the treatment of trauma. 'Sexuality for fulfilment. Sexology for understanding' read one of the little posters on the wall in my consulting room. Couples came to see me. I tried to get them to relax. That's what it's all about: relaxation. Clear the mind. Light the scented candles. Put on the mood music. In general, a couple's sexuality doesn't last long. It's no doubt due to their environment, to stress, et cetera. Take your lovemaking into new spaces. Even if it only means doing it in the living room rather than the bedroom, if you have a one-bedroom place. Men have no idea what to do with a clitoris, and women have no idea what to do with a penis. I knew. Romero was happy. The only problem was that I didn't like to be naked because of my scars. Anyway.

I showed drawings and anatomical cross-sections to the couples, my patients. I devised programs for them: gentle foreplay, sweet nothings to whisper. You have to be *in tune* with each other. Find a shared rhythm. Singing lessons are not a bad idea. Breathe in and breathe out. This part of my job often helped me clear my head.

Get a grip.

Where was I?

The final sessions with my clicker. I'd told him about my upcoming transplant, the eye exchange. That I would be away for about a week, so they could carry out the excision of my bad eye and replace it. He seemed to bristle a little. These stories must disgust him, I said to myself. 'An eye for an eye, a tooth for a tooth,' he said. I didn't understand. With enigmatic remarks like that, you'd have thought he was a shrink. He was wary of all forms of recording, even the routine ones done in the medical psychological centres. I said, 'So?' He said, 'Well, there you go.' And he started tapping beneath his eye, like when you want to tell someone to keep an eye out.

I was thirsty all the time. The kidney transplant

should have improved my condition. The doctors blamed the heatwave. But there was a heatwave every year. They told me to drink lots of water, but I was always thirsty. And as usual there were signs everywhere, all over the city and in the apartments, reminding us to stay hydrated. We were deluged with instructions, ha!

The persistent rumour that *there is something in the water* has always seemed to me like a conspiracy theory. But, session after session, my clicker refused every single glass of water I offered him, all of them. Silently, he produced his own flask. They were coming back into circulation, those metal flasks like the ones our grandparents took on camping trips. They made the water taste a bit salty. And, frankly, a bit like wine. Addresses of mineral springs and wine cellars were being passed around. As well as water filters to attach directly onto the tap. Well, anyway, that's what I started with, a pirated filter. It was my first course of action: basically, find something to drink.

Obtaining liquid supplies is a problem. Water storage takes up too much space. And you can't drink wine all day long—in my case, it stops me from working. I'm not trying to say there's some spectacular change once you stop drinking water, standard water. But, little by little, as you wean yourself off it, you feel things more intensely. Sometimes it even amounts to pain: it becomes unbearable to watch footage of the attacks, what with the organs, the blood. You have to close your eyes. Traumatic memories also return more vividly. And dreams. But good things too. Taste, for example. You become more discriminating, better at detecting factory-processed fruit—you can spot a strawberry from a plant that has actually been in the earth. And it's a more intense experience with other people, with nice people. I laugh at my clicker patient's jokes. I hold his gaze in silence.

When you stop drinking water, I mean the water delivered to us, it has the same effect in the long term as logging out. I suppose you've all tried to log yourselves out, for at least a few minutes, as my poor mother did inexpertly back when most of the devices remained on the outside of our bodies anyway. But it's possible to log out from inside as well. You just have to *find your interior chamber.* Don't think about anything at all, nothing, for a few minutes—this

91

starts to disrupt the connection. Don't respond to any requests, don't install any upgrades, don't process any data, don't react to any error even when it becomes unbearable, even when the problem morphs into physical pain. Get beyond that point. (I'm not saying it's easy.) Let your brain zone out. And find the source of the network within you. Unfortunately, with the rudimentary surgical equipment we have in the forest, my electrical box can't be removed. I'm not having anyone drill into my skull without some basic precautions. I don't want to be hacked to pieces like Apollinaire. (Apollinaire was a twentieth-century poet.) The nanny state we fled *occasionally* had its good points, like the precaution principle and state-of-the-art surgery. Anyway. The electrical box is still inside my head. 'A robot like the others.' But I manage to isolate it. Restrict it to its zone. I isolate its impulses. I'm used to its rhythm of trans-mission, and I ready myself. A bit like in martial arts: I return the energy to the adversary. Bit by bit, I'm sure I'm destroying the unit.

My clicker is not so sure. He really wants me to have it removed. He says if I keep it they'll be able to trip me out like a toaster. Finish me off remotely. I tell him that I'm falling to bits in any case, so there. Then we both collapse into each other's arms. Ha!

Where was I? I have to tell you everything about my clicker, I know. But before that: one of the first habits you have to lose in order to log out is to stop using your hands like computer mice. I know, it's difficult. Someone should write a story about it, I mean a historical story, on the cognitive function of our hands, how their function is linked to knowledge and to writing. Writing here in a notebook, and with only one hand (the right one, in my case), must surely have undone mental habits that were linked to the two-handed use of the keyboard, and to my two hands functioning as mice. To stop producing in space—like windmills—these never-ending repetitive actions of ignition and guidance of our devices, our headsets, our vehicles, for those who have them, our dogs, et cetera, is nothing less than a radical detoxification of our world. You exit the world. You end up in the forest, digging with shovels and picks. We stoke the braziers by blowing on them. We buttress the tunnels by hand, we fold the tents, we start all over again. We stir our stews ourselves, with a spoon. We scrub our dishes or we ask our halves to do it. We use our hands to hold objects.

The brain scans of people who log out reveal a brain that is fresher, with decreased and more evenly distributed activity: the image is more uniformly blue than red. The medial prefrontal cortex disconnects from the amygdala—that is, the ego centre is no longer linked to the fight-or-flight centre. It's also disconnected from the emotional centre (the ventromedial prefrontal cortex = thought processes, worries). These two areas of the cortex process information about people we consider similar to us (management of family relationships / depression), and people we consider different from us (management of social relations / anxiety). In a nutshell, we stop taking things too personally.

I've just remembered watching halves capering around in my psychology lessons. Once they're up on their feet, they caper around, literally. We have to come down hard on them. Halves learn quite quickly how to walk and to speak—and to read and to write, if we take the time to teach them (most of our halves are illiterate). Those adults who are woken up suddenly, however, are difficult to discipline. But our life in the forest calls for very strict regulation. And the halves only care about having fun. As if they wanted to catch up on all that time when they were asleep. All they think about is having sex, and the last thing we need is babies, so we sterilise as many of them as we can. Contrary to received opinion, clones *can* reproduce. Dolly the sheep (Dolly was the first mammal to be born not from a sperm and an egg, but from the transfer of a cell nucleus into an unfertilised egg cell) produced six biological lambs when she was bred with a Welsh mountain ram.

The main problem with clones seems to be their premature ageing. Take Dolly: her genetic material was already six years old when she was born. I have no idea how old mine is. I'm forty and I'm not going to be around for much longer, especially with the body parts I've lost. Marie's got a head start on me. They kept her in the Rest Centre, where she'd remain fresh and healthy, so they could use her for as long as possible after me. And it shows. She looks a lot more alive than I do. She has marvellous skin. And her innocence is marvellous too. I should have called her Dolly.

But when you go looking for information about

Dolly, you realise that perhaps, technically, she didn't die from being a clone. She died a stupid death, from lung cancer, not because she smoked too much (ha!) but because (if I remember correctly everything I've read about her since I understood what the deal was with me) she slept inside and not outside like ordinary sheep do. They kept her inside for fear of her being stolen. The first ever clone. And when they're inside, sheeps' lungs rot or whatever. She was also riddled with arthritis, and they blamed her old gene pool. But perhaps it was also because, just like our halves, she didn't get enough exercise. They didn't keep Dolly asleep, but they coddled her.

(I'm quoting all this from memory. In the forest, when an old clone dies, a whole library goes up in smoke. Ha!)

You should see our halves when we wake them up after the initial period on the stretchers. When they take their first steps, they're like newborn foals. And they have such pretty bodies, both the boys and the girls. It's hard to tell how old they are: you'd think they had stepped out of a painting of angels or nymphs, if that gives you any idea. And little by little their hair grows back. (We had a vote on whether to keep their heads shaved, for hygiene reasons; the no vote prevailed.)

Once a week, we take them for a compulsory swim in the river. Surreptitiously, we hold some cloth over the branches of a tree, to avoid the drones. We make them go in the river, otherwise they wallow in their own filth. We also teach them to swim. It's a whole palaver. A few of us have the exclusive task of looking after the halves, of keeping an eye on them, of training them (we deal with the most urgent cases). When we have time, we go along on their bathing days. There's a lot of laughter and squabbling and splashing around. It's delightful. You'd think you were at a holiday camp for adults. We dress them all in the same grey outfit—we found some bolts of fabric in a rubbish tip—pants and top, otherwise there's always the risk of treating the half as your owner. Well, we don't say 'owner', but we haven't found the right word yet. We're in discussion. Of course, when you see them all squatting together like a bunch of baboons, prattling away mindlessly, trying to be well-behaved, there's no way you would think they were us, the ones who have accumulated so many experiences, endured so many ordeals, overcome so many obstacles. But you never know. You never know what could be going through their minds. We tie them up at night, so they won't escape, or even—what a nightmare—go off and blow the whistle on us. We channel their energy by making them dig our tunnels. We have to teach them everything, even how to use a spade, but really, who among us still knows how to use a spade? We'd need more robots.

I'm cold.

I like Marie, that's not the problem. But I thought we'd be together forever. When they set her free, I couldn't stop holding her hands, kissing her, asking her if she was okay, what she wanted. And then I got sick of it. Or she rejected me, slowly but surely. She didn't want anything. That's the problem with halves. No, I mean, they do want lots of things: sugar, sex, food, sleep (as if they haven't slept enough!) and to hunt like cats (in the forest, the halves are our best procurers of protein). But really. No political sensibility at all, no metaphysical yearnings, no impetus towards the future. Everything's in the present for them. Admittedly, they don't have a past. It's hard to get your head around that. Some people expect us to show empathy for our halves. 'They're like us,' they say. But that kind of talk is hard to swallow. We're fed up with the old 'like us' drivel.

Well, anyway. Where was I? Back in the old days. When the clicker disappeared. I was really sad. Grief-stricken. After all, he was my patient zero. The one who taught me to stay silent. The substance of our most recent sessions left me hopeful, almost certain, that he had disappeared of his own accord. There was no trace, no body. But where would you disappear to, I asked myself? How would you do it? I was starting to be concerned about it, I guess. When he disappeared I sank into a deep depression. My eye operation was scheduled, which didn't help my morale. I'd been visiting Marie for years now, as often as I could, even during the state of emergency, and I had witnessed no progress whatsoever. It's stupid, but I think I'd started to confuse Marie with someone who was sick. Someone in a coma. Someone who could perhaps wake up one day. If I held her hand for long enough and if I said the right words to her. But no. There was no possibility of Marie waking up sometime in the future. No conceivable progress. It was very clear: Marie would remain asleep and at their disposal. Soon they were going to remove one of her eyes and transplant it into me.

I was seeing patients nonstop. Next. Next. I was so bored that I blinked discreetly, to change their position in my field of vision. I remember: I shut my left eye and saw them shift to the right. I shut my right eye and saw them shift to the left. I played around with it, moving them about. Watching them flatten or stand out in relief, eye closed, eye open. My eyes watered. I was the one who had to be given a tissue. Or a glass of water. Which I didn't drink. Yes, it was that period of my life: don't drink water = see my patients come and go before my eyes = keep waiting for the clicker who was not turning up = visit Marie, a lost cause = I almost had a breakdown. During the sessions with my patients, their words floated in space as if they had uttered them a long, long time ago. Floated and remained in the air. Floated and formed filaments that wove and spun together, and I wanted to escape, but I got caught in these hanging membranes, in these tapestries of no recognisable design. I stayed logged on the whole time during the sessions, in an effort to block it all out. Boredom is a sort of web in which you become entangled—a shroud, bandages. Yes, I was logged on during the sessions, which was wrong of me, and I received information from the outside world, offers for shopping bargains, sexual encounters, games, jokes, videos of atrocities or of cats. I kept on clicking and clicking, discreetly, moving my hand beneath my chair. In order to browse better, I tilted my head, discreetly. I blinked to pause on an image; the patients could think whatever they wanted. Some of them might have read approval or disagreement into it, but either way it sped up the session. Yet the boredom only became more intense, more speedy, it accelerated, I was trapped in a toboggan chute of boredom, a bobsled runway, a rocket in a tunnel. I was falling and at the end of the chute there was no firm ground, no ending, there was only a new window that opened onto a new window and new vistas. Well, you know the feeling.

Boredom is physical. You don't know how you're going to live the very next minute. You're supposed to fit your body somewhere, in space, but it's pointless. You're squashed inside the three stupid dimensions, and you wish you could disintegrate. You wish you could find the portal and pass into another dimension, one where you feel light and free, where any sensory stimulation would be like the air we breathe or the water we drink—I mean good water and good air. You wish you could swim like a fish in the water of the world. Fluid. In the gaps. Not stuck in the quicksand of time.

I waved the knitting needle that belonged to my mother—well, that person I thought was my mother—and my patients' eyes darted from side to side, and I envisaged us as flies, *bzzzz*. There was a smell of dead bodies. The patients knocked on the consulting-room door and I felt like asking them to help me. I should have. I'm sure they would've helped me; in fact they did help me when I was in pretty good shape. Perhaps it's paradoxical, but when I was doing well or just so-so, my patients shared in that wellness or so-so-ness. By seeking courageously how to live, they helped me to live. They were seeking solutions. It helped me to see them battle it out courageously. Come on, get a grip, I said to myself.

But now things were not going well. I couldn't stand my patients anymore. Their whingeing. Their obliviousness. Every time the door opened it was never my clicker. I suffered more frequent attacks of breathlessness. And then Wolf died. That dog was my only entertainment. My only companion. He died his dog's death, a natural death. He developed a classic case of clones' arthritis and respiratory failure and he began to suffer, like a dog. I had to come home every night to my dying dog...I suffered with him, I breathed with him, for him. I went to have him put down. It was dreadful. And straight afterwards I was supposed to have my operation. I wanted to delay it, so I could get over the death of my dog. But I needed to do better, as far as excuses go. We don't live in a world where the death of a dog can justify a change in the schedule.

There was, however, an incident before the operation. More than an incident, but at the time I didn't know what to do about it. A pigeon. It came and perched at the window of my consulting room. I like to go to work because it gets me out of my studio, and also because in my consulting room there's that little window. You can see outside. The pigeon wouldn't leave. I was afraid it would shit everywhere and make a mess of the wall. We already get into enough trouble for things like that, so I wanted to shoo it away. It had a sort of little pipe instead of a claw. A mutant, I said to myself, but no, it was a little tube. Hollow. The bird allowed itself to be handled, as if that was exactly what it was waiting for. I opened the tube. Inside was a piece of rolled-up paper, a handwritten note: 'Deprogram yourself. It's blindingly obvious.'

It seemed like the pigeon was waiting for an answer. It was looking at me with its round eye, one side, then the other, *click, click,* moving its head as if it was on a spring. I didn't know what to write. I was paralysed. I had to hope that the images from this incident would not be viewed for a good while. I let the pigeon fly away. Dumb bird.

They performed the operation to remove my eye.

I was in incredible pain and the horse tranquillisers made me dizzy. The pain fried half my head, radiating from under the crown of my head down to my jaw. It'll pass, they told me. Wait until they take off your dressings. In the meantime, no touching! The physiotherapy would begin later. The wound had to heal over first.

In the meantime, it was exhausting only seeing

out of one eye. I tilted my head the whole time, like the pigeon. I wanted everything to fit into my field of vision, so I could see the big picture and ease my pain.

I went to see Marie. It was always my first instinct. My solution when things weren't going well. When I didn't have a clue about anything. But they did make a point of commenting at the Rest Centre, and even at work. You'd have thought they were in cahoots, coming up with the same line: 'All those trips have made you tired.' I was coughing. And there they all were with their glasses of water. Water, my arse!

I had braced myself to see her with a dressing over her eye, like me. Since she'd given me her eye. Or they'd taken her eye. Right? 'Why doesn't she have a dressing?' I asked them. Only the nurses were there. 'Blah, blah, we don't know,' they replied. (No, I'm kidding, they didn't say *blah, blah*. They replied normally.) Well, whatever, they were programmed to keep quiet.

Under that closed eyelid, so serene, was there perhaps a gaping hole? A bloody eye socket?* Needless to say, I wasn't allowed to touch, to feel if it

---

* I've no longer got time to check if this is the correct word.

was soft. So I sat next to Marie. I leaned over. And did that trick I never did anymore. I whispered in her ear in an authoritative tone. There's never any point to it, other than seeing the terror it triggers in their eyes. Although, you know, some of them like it.

So I sat next to Marie and I murmured in her ear, 'Deprogram. It's blindingly obvious.'

Or something like that. It's the tone that's important. Not what you say.

Her eyes snapped open. Both eyes. Terrified. She had both her eyes.

'It's a glass eye,' the doctor told me once I'd managed to get hold of him. 'We put her real eye in a culture so it will be in perfect condition for you. We'll let you know as soon as it's ready.'

Did he think he was preparing some mouth-watering dish?

I'd never heard of anything like it. Seriously, this doctor seemed to be flying by the seat of his pants. With my lung, and with my kidney, they'd transplanted them straightaway. It was simple: they put me to sleep alongside Marie, side by side in the operating room, and, hey presto, the transplant went from one body to the other. The organs leaped from one stretcher to the other. That's the image I've always had in my mind, from the way they've talked about it since I was a very little girl.

'How did you see that she had both her eyes?' the doctor asked me in an accusatory tone. 'I hope you didn't *touch* her eyes?' So I told him about the trick where you whisper to them in an authoritative tone. He seemed to find that incredibly mouth-watering.

I returned home, troubled.

I didn't buy the line about the glass eye. Even if it's true that they make excellent replicas here. I had seen her eyes, her two animate eyes. Lightning-fast, but her animate eyes, definitely. Perhaps her eye was indeed going to be cut out for me, but later? Surely there must have been an incident report?

It wouldn't have been difficult to put a dressing on her eye. To fool me so I'd wait. Pretty neat way of fooling me. Fancy dress for her, in a way. Couldn't they show me a bit more respect, after all? Spin me a more satisfactory lie? All I needed was an explanation. All I needed was to be told or not told, but not some grey area in between. If you get my drift. I was losing my bearings, reeling. I couldn't see clearly at all, if you'll allow me to be so literal. Perhaps they were starting to realise we found it appalling that they chopped pieces out of our halves. Perhaps they were frightened we'd protest, like my mother did.

I had dreams in which I was eating Marie. I began with a finger; it was tasty, so I grew bolder. I continued up her hand, to her arm; it was bleeding and I panicked at the idea that all this blood was going to mean the end of my transplant deal. I woke up with a start, turned on the light and my studio was still divided in two. I still had to twist my neck around to see the whole room. To check there was no one crouched in the shadows.

They treat us like cattle, I told myself. They infantilise us to the point of not informing us about our procedures, even when it's *our* bodies! *My* body!

I sounded like my mother when she got angry, the poor thing. My body, my arse.

After I'd made my stupid disclosure to the doctor, the robot nurses were programmed to monitor us closely. It was now absolutely forbidden to whisper in the ear of the halves. We had to comply with their sleep regime. Those who got a kick out of waking them up gave me dirty looks. My friends. I wanted to say to them: so what, since our halves always fall back to sleep afterwards?

Come on!

A terrible time.

I went to see my supervisor. I needed him. I needed to tell him about my dreams, and my eye, and Marie, and the transplant deferment, and Marie's eye in the culture and her glass eye supposedly replacing it. My dreams and visions were like quicksand. I woke in the morning to see a single eye in a storage jar, growing, swelling, and all of reality—the patients, the tram, my studio, the neighbour's plants that kept on dying—got mixed into a culture broth, full of filaments, which was the air itself I was trying to breathe.

'*Hmmm,*' said my supervisor (that's what old-school shrinks always say). '*Hmmmmmmm.* Glass eye. Does that make you think of something?'

I tried to associate, but nothing came to mind.

'Ah, no,' I said.

'*Hmmmmm,*' he said.

When it was time for my next session, my supervisor didn't open the door. Three days later, when I placed a query against his name in my device, I found out that he'd died. Terminal cancer.

Terminated, I said to myself.

So I took off my dressing. I had the devil of a time. It was stuck! It hurt like hell! But I wanted to see. As if taking off the dressing would restore my vision. But dressing or no dressing, I still only saw out of one eye. And as far as seeing goes, I was in for a shock: they had also removed my eyelids. Instead of an eye, there was a scar, not exactly a scar, more like a tight seam, a black thread that sutured the eyebrow to the cheekbone.

I was unrecognisable.

I stuck the dressing back on, a perfect disc of white adhesive gauze.

I was in two minds about asking the doctor from the Centre to clarify, once and for all, the exact date of my future transplant. Would Marie be disfigured in the same way? I didn't want them to do that to her. No, I really didn't want that. Even in order to regain a human face.

I'd been mulling over the pigeon's message and suddenly I thought: Honey, if you keep asking, if you put pressure on them, you're going to disappear too. You will be disappeared. I had a lightbulb moment. An 'insight', shrinks would call it. Things fell into place. The pieces of the puzzle. You're going to disappear like Romero did after he put in a request for teeth. You're going to disappear like Romero did after he'd filled in the request form to schedule his operation. What he scheduled was his termination.

I understood. At least I understood part of what was going on. I hadn't yet worked it all out—that if I was constantly breathless and constantly thirsty, it wasn't so much that the air was polluted and that I was going without water, it was that I had only one lung left, and only one kidney left. I hadn't yet understood that.

Today, I need to write. I don't know if it does me any good to write, but I can see. I see what they're doing to us. I feel it. With the rest of my body.

I'm lying under the trees as I write, my back against a mound of earth. I'm making an effort to breathe slowly. It's a sunny day, even if we always stay in the shade. Every now and again I tip my head back and try to concentrate on the foliage. With my head upside down, and my single eye, I try to see things from the other side, as they say. You can't feel the wind at ground level, and the trees above seem to be moving by themselves. They're swaying their arms, their branches; they're waving their green hands; they're doing the helicopter. I try to empty my mind. To breathe. The air is marvellous here. It smells green. It smells like sap. It's so good. Between the leaves, I glimpse confetti pieces of sky. Sequins of sky. It's raining blue sky. The blue sky settles over me.

Pope Francis was a twenty-first-century pope who lived with only one lung. It's possible. Even without faith. He suffered from serious pneumonia when he was young and underwent a pneumonectomy, the removal of a lung. He died when he was very old, and was quite a good man. He looked after the poor. He breathed as well as he could, but managed to travel a lot, et cetera. Not like me. But that's neither here nor there.

I digress.

Let's get back to it.

My dog died but another dog arrived. A stray. They exist here. They even gather in packs on the outskirts of the cities. I had never come across any around the Centre, but I think they terminate them en masse out there. It was one of those yellow dogs with dirty matted hair, the result of a long series of interbreeding between dogs of all sorts of species. Some pretty serious, non-stop mixing. It was waiting at the bottom of my building. This dog without a human seemed odd, given that it had a collar—not exactly a collar, but a thin cord around its neck. The thinnest piece of cigarette paper was rolled around the cord. Written on the paper were the words: 'Disappear *now*.'

How do you go about disappearing? How do you do it? I was happy enough to log out, but that meant ending up completely alone, without money, without a home—when you connect, it links you to the front door of your residence. You forget exactly how much every single one of our movements is networked, recorded, categorised, et cetera. Read by robots. Archived, measured, indexed. That totally ordinary action of opening your front door by identifying yourself with your hand. Of paying by simply passing through a security gate with an iris scanner (and it works with only one eye). Of telephoning by simply activating the microphone in your ear. You forget all that. When you disappear, I thought, you can't do anything any longer. You can't exist any longer. You're lost in limbo, trapped between two blades of time. I told myself that I had to stop using my body as an interface. But how?

Later on, I learned that in the forest they collect organs, especially hands and eyes. They retrieve them from fresh cadavers. They work it out. They trade. I don't have anything to do with that, but I know it's the first step in any identity jamming. Basic stuff. But I'd been hacked about and tinkered with enough to accept the transplant of a hand belonging to someone else, alive or dead.

I was reconciled to losing everything when I disappeared. I stockpiled whatever I could, like food—energy bars, that sort of thing. A water filter. Last of all, I put on sturdy, comfortable, warm clothes. And my mother's checked raincoat. I dug up some well-made shoes. A space blanket. I told my patients that I had some post-operative complications and had to take a leave of absence.

As well as the unit in my head, I have two implants like everyone else: one under the skin of my forearm, and one under my ear, and that's not counting the Centre's ID tag under the skin on my wrist. It's not difficult to remove, but (I'm giving you a heads-up) it hurts. It's been embedded there since

I was a child. The various tissues are difficult to cut through; there's a lot of blood. And for the forearm or the wrist, you have to grab the skin between your teeth to be able to operate with the other hand.

It's painful, but it has to be done. Get some help if you don't have the nerve to do it. I didn't have anyone I could count on—my mother was dead, as well as Romero, and the old woman upstairs… I scarcely knew the nice neighbours, apart from when we'd all helped the old woman. You never know who will denounce you. You never know who will shoot the wretched in the dungeons. I think it's possible to find out a bit about someone from looking into their eyes, or from the very first words they say—you can find out on first meeting them, or, on the contrary, after a very long time. But back then I didn't even know how to trust myself. I believed everything I was told.

I put on a scarf to hide the wound under my ear. The sleeves of the raincoat covered the cuts on my arms. I hopped on a train without a ticket and slid my device into the pocket of a cleaning robot, who would make a few round trips before anyone became worried about someone as deficient as me going missing, about my minuscule dot on the radar systems. So off I went. Into the forest.

The dog from the bottom of the building followed close at my heels, and stayed with me. He jumped in the train I'd caught at random. Not exactly at random, because that train followed the tram route, then went on further and entered the section of the forest where the Rest Centre was located. I got off among the trees, in a field that seemed promisingly empty. The dog followed me. And then he no longer followed me, but went ahead. And we walked together for a long time. It was spring and I hadn't even noticed. One of those rare days of true spring in a once temperate area, a day that was neither freezing nor stifling hot, a cool, sunny day with a light and gentle wind that touches your face like—I can't think of a comparison—like a caress. I took off my scarf. The wind caressed the wound under my ear. I could feel the cells working hard to heal over. It was good.

The forest was astonishing. Tiny little bright-green leaves, a green so natural that it looked artificial, the green you think of when you think of green: tiny little leaves growing at the ends of absolutely every single branch. I wanted to touch them, to be touched by this foliage that was soft and velvety and so green. And I couldn't hear anything apart from the sound of the wind in the trees, and occasionally, yes, a bird. Astonishing. I was trembling, breathing, no tension, nothing. Just the call of the wind, the trees and the birds, and the sun. And of the dog, whom I was following, and who had the tact to act as if he was following me.

Standing under a tree was the clicker.

We set off walking like beasts of burden. Despite the fresh air, the effort made me short of breath. We had to keep stopping. We'd run out of water and the next spring was a long way off. 'Get a grip,' said the clicker. We burst out laughing. Yes, he managed to make me laugh. We were laughing because that's what I used to say to him all the time, when he was my patient. It's what I used to say to all my patients. He squinted and I was overcome by the sight of his face in the sun, and our three eyes continued to look at each other.

'They didn't go easy on you,' he said.

We set off again.

Dog and I were together for a long time. He

was the first dog I'd had who was called Dog. He belonged to the clicker and me, in the sense that he was happy enough to stay with us.

The first days in the encampment I was intoxicated. Sure, my reduced vision unbalanced me, but mostly it was being out in the open. Getting up in the morning and stepping out of the tent, and, hey presto, there was the forest, the clearing. The earth. Just a few steps and I was out in the sunshine. Back under the trees, barefoot, to wash in the river. The wide-open spaces. When I arrived, there were a number of people—for security reasons I can't say how many—including a few halves. It was the halves' job to dig the dry toilets. It's fair to say that those toilets made a big improvement in the general hygiene of the group.

We fugitives were going to retrieve our halves as soon as we could. At first I thought everyone was similarly motivated: the same nostalgia that I felt, being away from Marie for so long. So long without being able to touch her, speak to her, so long dealing with her just sleeping. I thought we all wanted to find our halves because we missed them. Things are actually more complicated. I'm coming around to thinking that we each have a different story with our halves.

Anyhow, when I arrived, an attack had been staged against a small provincial centre: a blackout was triggered, during which ten or so halves had been retrieved and transported in a truck. They're still only one-off operations, said the clicker. Amateurism like that annoyed him. A much grander plan was being hatched: to empty the Rest Centre completely. They were camping in the forest to prepare their attack.

I couldn't take my eye off the few halves who had recently been reanimated. Their gestures were clumsy, not like children's, more like adult-children, horses who had sprung in one go from being foals to being fully grown mares, without learning anything in between. They limped but they were lively. They ran around as fast as their legs could carry them, but got themselves in a muddle. They fell down laughing. They tussled with each other, they got told off, they set out again with their buckets to do the chores.

The clicker and I had a lot of serious conversations. The therapy framework had prevented us from talking to each other. We were catching up. He spoke to me about the Sioux. (The Sioux were

Native Americans, many of whom were killed in the eighteenth and nineteenth centuries.) The teepees in the forest were inspired by their dwellings, especially the ventilation system with rotating deflectors. The clicker could talk about them for hours. You had to be able to dismantle a teepee in less than half a day. Otherwise, you abandon everything. They had already done that a few times. Which was precisely why many members of the group were lobbying for another means of escape: by living in underground tunnels.

My clicker was disgusted by the idea. 'We are not moles,' he said. But this way of thinking was gaining traction and the halves were corralled into digging holes, tunnels, a whole complicated system of underground dwellings, less movable but more permanent, where we could stay hidden for longer. Our leader drew up the plans (the clicker wasn't the leader). He delivered us lectures of sorts, on marmots. When you study the burrows of marmots from earlier times, there is a main hibernation room, adjoining storage rooms, and a little room at quite a distance, at the end of a long tunnel: the toilet. On the sand at the edge of the river, he drew cross-section plans of a semi-permanent encampment.

The halves chopped wood and buttressed the tunnels until they collapsed with exhaustion. In the clicker's opinion, too much energy was expended on the tunnels; he wanted us back on the road. But how could we set off again inconspicuously if we were forever animating new halves? We had to get them on their feet and train them, et cetera. Some among us actually thought that, with this workforce, we could build an alternative, underground city, in competition with the connected city, et cetera. That we could establish ourselves there. For the future. There were a lot of arguments.

For now, we wrapped ourselves in camouflage material whenever we were out in the open. The leaders' teepees were made of all-weather fabric, when we could find it; the clicker even had a little bottle of plasma spray that would, if necessary, conceal his escape. He was going to get me one too.

The hundred-odd halves at the Centre was nothing, he told me, when you consider that one to two per cent of human beings have at least one clone. Those who are less rich have jars with a simple heart–lungs operating system, and the vast majority of other human beings are superfluous, without purpose, and therefore, needless to say, without doubles or any sort of jar. It's a very easy population pie chart to draw. According to the clicker, there was a huge market in organs that had been *snatched* from random bodies, kidnapped, and the compatibility tests on the transplant were carried out haphazardly; the organ lasted only as long as it lasted, and the cycle began again. Obviously it cost a lot less than a clone. *I* was expensive. That made him laugh. Ha! But what cost the most was Marie. I was already a second-hand model. That made him laugh and laugh! A few birds were singing and we were walking under our camouflage capes, making our way slowly back to the encampment. He lifted up the canvas of his teepee for me. All we needed was a dry bed, a warm blanket, drinking water and grains and vegetables. So the clicker told me. Look where progress got us. And we talked and talked and kissed and hugged each other. We caught up on lost time.

Where was I?

I have to hurry.

The clicker loved me right down to my scars.

He persuaded me to live without the dressing, to take off this thing that came from them. But I was too ugly without the dressing. I looked like I'd died by a thousand cuts. I didn't recognise myself. So I just tied a scarf around my eye. No problem at all: they nicknamed me the Pirate. The Clicker and the Pirate. The new Bonnie and Clyde. (Bonnie and Clyde were a couple of famous outlaws in the twentieth century.)

His own half had disappeared. He didn't say much about it. He hadn't coped well discovering he had a double. It's quite an unusual experience all the same, he'd say to me. Even if it happens to a lot of us. Right? He coped very badly with it.

Well, there you go.

He wanted to set the halves free. It was his big thing, his big idea.* Then, he imagined, we'd have an army of sleeping soldiers. He told me about an army of terracotta soldiers, buried somewhere in China in antiquity, and that a breath of wind could wake them, reanimate the rows and rows of them

--------

* I helped him, thanks to the two weapons hidden at Romero's place.

to walk on the ground...Our halves are like that, he said. We need to train them. Arm them.

I'll spare you the discussions all this provoked in the group. My clicker quoted Russian writers and the others told him to go to hell. *We were few in number, and what's more, we were not united.** There was only a handful of us, and when I say a handful I have an image of a closed fist, between whose pitiless fingers skeletal bodies are contorting, trying to escape.

That's the image I have in my mind.

I'm cold. I had to stop writing because I had trouble breathing. Water is dripping into the tunnels. The deepest ones have become uninhabitable; there's been too much rain lately.

And yet it is possible, I assure you, to live like nomads.

We were all in agreement about setting the halves free, but we disagreed about what to do with them, about the long-term plan, about whether to flee or to stay and fight. We had no idea. In the end, was it

---

* Variation on a quotation from the Russian writer Alexey Rybnikov.

up to us? Is one free in a forest? It's early days, some said. We battled it out and we drank.

The halves crouched in a circle around us and pinched our grog and bits of rat. They laughed. They watched us arguing. Then, in the glow of the embers, they had sex. We didn't manage to sterilise everyone—too many halves and not enough equipment. There was the issue of babies. The last thing we wanted in the forest was to lug around babies, especially the babies of halves. I don't know why it was the women who had to sort this out. I was disgusted by the whole baby thing. So I was criticised. And then you had to do self-criticism, otherwise you got into big trouble. It was interminable. It's easy to disappear in the forest too.

Anyway.

I can't really enlarge upon our life in the forest. It's a matter of security.

I wasn't directly involved in the escape plan for the halves, so I can only recount what I know, cautiously, according to what my clicker was willing to tell me about it. (I say 'my' clicker: you'll understand that it's a mark of affection, not of appropriation.) I was in a bad way, and too short of breath to take part in an operation like that.* My only task was to keep a close eye on the halves who had already been rescued and gathered into various small units. I've never really liked children, and halves are worse. As it was night, they were supposed to sleep, each one attached to the stake alongside their straw mattress, underground. But they made an infernal racket and there were only a few of us acting as guards until the expedition returned. I was frightened a traitor would turn up, that someone would take this opportunity to attack us or whatever. I get claustrophobic in the tunnels. We listened out for noises in the night. We hit the halves to make them shut up. What would be the upshot of all that, I wondered. In the short term, it was a long night.

On this particular night, our group had organised a sort of train. Not exactly a train, but one of those vehicles you see on railway tracks, a handcar, used in the past for maintenance, I think, a *draisine*. There was one there on the disused track. They

---

* I'm not trying to justify myself about anything, but I'd like to point out again that if I didn't take an *active* part in this operation, I provided logistical support, as well weapons (two).

brought it back and tinkered with it. They attached a trailer that we nicknamed the Raft because it was made out of logs of wood that had been only roughly squared off, on which we had mounted side boards and attached vines in anticipation of a load. They selected two halves, two strapping fellows built like removalists, whom they trained for two days on this carriage. They all sprayed themselves with plasma and wrapped themselves in strips of camouflage material. Our two armed robots were going off with them. It was impossible to trigger an electrical blackout in such a major Rest Centre: there were generators and powerful batteries. So our group kept it simple. They set off in search of gas masks, and even cobbled them together from lichen and scraps of electrically resistant material. I witnessed all the preparations.

Am I talking too much? Am I writing too much?

Let's just say that when they came back, the Raft was full of piled-up bodies. Our halves. My clicker had the genius idea of severing the gas lines that were keeping the halves asleep. The gas spread everywhere. Hilarious. Ha! The robots were the only ones not to get knocked out. So I immediately had to know who was a robot and who wasn't; I wanted to know if the doctor who had operated on me was one, if the guy who had chatted me up about my eye was one. But my clicker hadn't had time to identify them. We weren't there for that, he said. We were there to set the halves free. Our pirated robots shot at the nurse robots—I liked the idea of frying their brain cells. But the hardest thing was carrying the halves to the Raft. We had planned for two humans per half, one at the shoulders, the other with the legs. It was slow going. They had only managed to free about fifty per cent of the halves. All piled up on the Raft. An epic saga in the forest. They woke up, eyes staring wide, distraught, incapable of the slightest action, unable to get themselves moving. Sometimes I wonder if robots, in the end…know themselves. The most sophisticated robots. The clones who've just been woken up are the only ones left who don't know themselves at all. Unless they dream. Perhaps. Perhaps they've lived something in their sleep, after all.

I've added this detail because I know it has raised a lot of questions: on this expedition we rescued two halves without owners. I mean two solitary halves.

The one belonging to Mathias Matéo, my classmate who disappeared (and there he was, all of a sudden: unchanged, juvenile, semi-idiotic), and José, the half belonging to the husband of my suicide patient, you know, the miracle sole survivor of the crash. José never integrated well. He always remained alone, without the husband. We never really succeeded in getting José up and walking, adapting him to camp life, to work, to digging—well, to his life as a half. He spent his time whistling, stupidly staying out in the open to watch drones and—I'm not kidding— making little planes out of balsa wood, which he flew in the wind on strings.

I have to hurry.

At first, I wanted to tame Marie, keep her for myself. I knew her, she didn't know me. Or perhaps she did have a vague, intuitive knowledge of me? I wanted to live with her in the same teepee, and, later, in the same hole. No one else did that. But I thought it was discriminatory to herd our halves together in what amounted to a *dormitory*. One evening I even called our group a pack of bastards. I slept with Marie. But in the morning, as soon as she woke up, she went running off to join the other halves. I'd

129

taught her to speak: 'Marie, Viviane, you, me, eat, drink, sleep...' (Halves never want to sleep at the right time.) But she never told me anything. She went off to prattle with the other halves—I was going to say with halves like her. It had taken me two months to teach her to walk, and she still fell flat on her face all the time. And two months to teach her to talk. In the beginning, she sat still obediently and imitated me, repeating my words. All in one go, all of a sudden, they can start speaking fully formed sentences. Their brain is that of an adult and they've been immersed in language, even when they were asleep. But their muscles, lips, tongue, et cetera, are stiff. The nurses worked on engaging the legs and arms but not the face—I have no idea why. I've always suspected that, if the need arose, they wouldn't rule out the idea of waking up this whole mute army. Anyway. Once Marie managed to pronounce words, she had nothing to say. All she wanted to do was go and see Pépette and Mathias Mark 2 and the others. And when I insisted that she come back 'before midnight', she sulked and didn't tell me anything. Did you have a good time? Nothing. Do you want some blackberries?

Nothing. Well, anyway. We put her to work.

Still, you could say that I saved her. You could say that she even owes me her life. They would have chopped her up like all the rest, so the only thing left of me would have been a carcass, which they would have recycled as dog food.

One of the first things I did—I mean, as soon as I was able to—was to undress her. Remove her isolation bubble of hypoallergenic material. When you're taking off their clothes they're passive, relaxed. It even excites them sometimes. Marie is still intact. Intact all over. José has some scars. That's probably why he has a screw loose. He's also missing a testicle, as the clicker pointed out to me. We might have intervened just in time, before they removed everything from him. Before they terminated him even. In the end it's turned out well, that the husband of my suicide patient was pulverised in the sky. He avoided any organ removal. *Crash!* A form of release, freedom! I don't know if Mathias Mark 2 is missing a few bits, but he tends to run away as soon as you go near him. The solitary halves, like him and José, are in the firing line. Like us. We are the disposable bodies, the first bodies to jettison.

Marie is still pretty, even with her regulation grey outfit. Dishevelled hair, always full of straw or something or other. A disarming smile. Her lips a bit chapped from the fresh air and the cold. I wanted to take care of her. She didn't want me to. She thrashed around in my arms, like a flighty filly.

I gave up. And anyway, my clicker was jealous. We shared the same teepee (while we were living in teepees). He was a sane man, my clicker. An honest man, loyal and loving. A true resistance fighter. He told me that I aroused him, with my newly released half in the same bed.

I think it's hard to love someone who has a half. Who the hell knows what he's done with his half? And the ones who've got jars don't have the same deal as us at all. They don't turn into fugitives. They're happy to admit that they have replacement hearts and lungs, available in a goddam storage jar, and there you go. It must even be quite a reassuring thought. Statistically, it prolongs life by a dozen or so years, which is nothing to sneeze at. In any case, loving someone who *is* a half (that's what we should say, but I can't get used to it)—well, it's not that straightforward. I'll leave it up to you—to your common sense, to your imagination—to envisage the consequences of a situation like this. You're perfectly capable of it. With a bit of empathy. A bit of sympathy. I can't do everything, in this notebook. I'm running out of steam. I've already written one hundred and thirty-three pages. And then, well, if you're still up for it, you'll draw your own conclusions. I can't do more than that.

I'm cold.

I have to hurry.

I'm lying down at the end of a tunnel. They've wrapped me in woollen material and moss. Halves are bringing me down hot herbal tea. We've run out of wine. I'm coughing. I can't get enough air. But we're being hunted down. I'd like to go outside and breathe. I'd like to breathe like a normal mammal endowed with two lungs. A kind half found me an old pot of honey. I don't see Marie anymore. I don't know what's happening to her. Sissy never visits me. The bitch.

I'd like to write 'we wrapped me in woollen material', because it's *our* group, *us* who are looking after *me*. But, oddly enough, you can't write that. Not in any language, as far as I know. I have no

133

choice but to write 'they…me', not 'we…me'. I'm learning. I've been writing for a fair while now, but I'm still discovering things. If I wasn't writing, I'd be wondering what I'm doing here, in this hole, with this group. Sometimes, I'm completely surprised. In the old days, babies born by caesarean section were called 'surprised babies'. Because they hadn't battled to get out of their mothers' bodies. Because they hadn't endured the contractions. They were born without transitioning.

Where was I? I stopped writing for a bit because Moses flipped out. We had to deal with him. Moses had huge expectations for our big expedition and he hasn't got over his disappointment. They didn't manage to bring him back his half, Momo. At first I thought Moses was attached to Momo like I was to Marie, and I was upset for him, for his suffering. Moses would talk to himself under the trees. He raised his head to the sky and stood holding his chest. The clicker told me that, at the very instant our team was about to grab Momo, a group of nurses behaved in an unusually heroic way. They began to defend the dormitory as if their lives depended on it. As if they really and truly believed in the whole thing. As if together they had decided to counter-attack. It was terrifying. They lined up and used their bodies like battering rams, charging at our team. A hellbent robot is like a speeding truck that nothing can stop. Our team took flight. And they left Momo back there. Unplugged. All alone. No one knows what happened to him.

I felt sorry for Moses, but as it turns out he is part of a small group of people I'm wary of. I haven't worked out exactly what's going on, but it's a group that works at some distance from our tunnels. They've organised a field hospital operating theatre. Moses is at the end of his life, like me. He has a heart condition on top of everything else. And I think he had designs on Momo's heart.

We can't let things like that happen. Can we? In my mind, we were reuniting—I mean, we were rescuing our halves simply to be with them. To protect them. So that they wouldn't suffer what was happening to us. If we too start chopping them up— that's not good.

The expedition also got hold of some old jars stockpiled at the Centre, and still full. One solution that came up was to collect a reasonably fresh heart from one of the jars and attempt a transplant on Moses, to console him, in a way. Personally, I wouldn't go near a heart whose provenance or removal date was unknown. Anyway, the whole group is arguing and arguing about it; before it goes to a vote, Moses will have had time to drop dead ten times over. I can understand why he's lost it.

When I arrived at the forest, my clicker showed me some videos. At first I thought they were advertisements, ads for a better world, for holidays or something like that. Old people at the beach. A sea unlike any I'd set eyes on. I've only ever seen the sea once, on a school excursion. It was overcast and raining, but that wasn't what annoyed me; it was that I couldn't actually see the sea. I would have liked to get a bit more perspective. We were level with the water, flat water on a flat beach, and I would have had to climb up to a high spot, but there we were, shuffling around on that narrow beach. All I could see was a band of grey water with some sky above. I thought the sea was much bigger. What do you see when you see the sea? Only a fragment. I wanted to see the *whole* sea. Anyway. On the video you can see old people on a white beach with overhanging trees that provide what seems like the most lovely shade, and a turquoise sea, utterly turquoise, neither blue nor green but that colour you see on pigeons' throats...sometimes, on some pigeons...well, anyway, I'm making a comparison with whatever I can. With the colour of my eyes. On the video the old people are laughing and cuddling each other and passing suncream around and drinking from tall coloured glasses and sleeping and listening to music and doing the kinds of things you'd imagine doing in a world where you didn't have to work all the time or look for work that didn't exist and worry about how you were going to pay for everything that had to be paid for and fight off all the illnesses and all the pain and when you got home deal with a dog that wasn't even a dog. I began to understand that it wasn't an ad because not a single product was being pitched—apart from the old people them-selves, in a way, the lifestyle of old people. I began to feel angry. It wasn't a holiday resort, or a luxury retirement home, not exactly. It was their life. The clicker zoomed in on one woman in particular. The hologram image magnified, and magnified, and I hiccupped. I couldn't breathe properly anymore. I tried to breathe, to breathe, catch my breath, but it didn't come, I couldn't inhale, on the contrary every-thing inside me wanted to disgorge itself, the hiccup turned into nausea. It was a stolen video—the clicker had obtained it through our undercover network—but the hologram was high-definition and the woman looked at me with eyes that I recognised. I recognised her. She was old, but they were my eyes. It was me.

It was me as a very old woman. That seemed strange for a start. The image had been doctored, altered, enlarged, the wrinkles photoshopped out, but it was an old woman who was identical to me. Me when I would never reach that age. Because I'm going to die soon, with what's left of my body. That's why I'm in a hurry to write.

Have to hurry.

Her face…The worst was looking at her eyes. That quite unusual green verging on turquoise, with a golden halo around the pupil. A narrow scar circled her left eye. It was attractive, like a smile line, but I'm sure that scar annoyed her—when we zoomed in you could see she tried to hide it with concealer. It was an attractive scar. It had turned out well. She had not only taken my eye but also my eyelids, my attractive eyelids, still smooth, transplanted onto that face stranded somewhere beyond time. With my rows of eyelashes, with my tear duct. An eye like the sea, the sea where she cavorted like a happy-go-lucky sea lion. What did she see? I saw the sea she saw. It was my eye, my missing eye. I had a feeling in my belly, something black like bile, icy-cold. I'm frightened, I thought. That's it. She frightens me. She is terrifying, horrendously so. Pure horror. So I thought: Get a grip. The feeling rose from my belly towards my throat. I felt hot in the head, in my cheeks, even my brain felt hot. Have you ever felt like killing someone? I mean for real, not metaphorically? When you work out in practical terms how you're going to go about it, which flight you'll need to catch, the location, the hideout, the weapon, your ways and means, accomplices, the level of suffering you want to inflict before death?

The clicker told me she was probably about a hundred and sixty years old. On the video, when you see them up close, the old people are more or less old. In spite of the plastic surgery, you can see from the wrinkled bodies that some of the old people are about eighty, while others must be heading for two hundred. All of them are white—I mean, tanned from the sun, but white. Judging from the average age of those old, rich creatures, whom we call (so the clicker told me) the *pureblood stock,* there isn't just one but several Generations, so instead of referring to halves, we have to say thirds or quarters, probably even tenths. They use one clone, then two, then three, then four, et cetera. They dissect them one after the other. What's more, a lot of those purebloods have had biological children, who themselves were entitled to their doubles or to their triples, not just to the jars of organs given to those who are, let's say, simply well off. Only the planet's super-rich can afford clones.

The clicker zoomed in on the very old and very well-preserved body of my pureblood. I could just make out another narrow scar below her right breast, below the bikini top, right where my lung was breathing, right where my heart would be beating if they captured me, where Marie's heart was beating or that of other thirds and quarters I didn't even know, younger ones, stored away or hidden somewhere. Purebloods can have their heart replaced—

or any organ they want—several times in their lives. Almost indefinitely. Kidneys, liver, stomach, veins, arteries, eyes, genitals…Entire sections of skin can also be transplanted, it works well, like clothing made of skin, smooth bellies, thighs, faces, arms… But it's expensive to have a clone, even for the one per cent of super-rich who own ninety-nine per cent of the world's wealth. Breeding a clone costs them about one per cent of their ninety-nine per cent—I'll let you be the judge. So, when the egg is good, it's more economical to do it in pairs. When the egg is good, as in the case of almost all my Generation, they harvest it straightaway, divide it and implant it in two or more uteruses. My mother was never more than my incubator. That woman huddled inside her raincoat, hunched over her knitting or craning towards her virtual images, crouching against the gate to the Centre. Sometimes such a rebel. My mother.

That's how they came up with Marie and me, and all the others, Momo and Moses, and José and my patient's husband, and Pépette and Juliette, et cetera. And they had a shot at that experiment of keeping one asleep, who didn't wear out, and to let the other one loose in the jungle of the world. The pairs of twins drove the scientists crazy. One's looking for work and accommodation, while the other one lies snoring in a space blanket. I swear you'd think it was a reality TV show. Social peace, they call it. They tried heaps of things. Personally, I think it's the demon of comparison at work. I'd rather not know. Honestly.

My clicker sensed that I was weakening. He held me tight. He tried to make me laugh. And he succeeded, the idiot. The trauma is in the past, he said. The baby you once were no longer exists, even its *cells* no longer exist. The past is past. You must live completely in the present. Know who you are! Focus on your timeline! Treat your old wounds like contaminating agents to be cleansed from your system! *Where's the baby?*

They were the same words I used to chant to my patients. That I used to chant to him. And now he was playing peekaboo with me. *Where's the baby?* We got the giggles.

I don't even know if it's the multimillionaire old biddy who is directly responsible for my fate. For my birth—let's say it like it is. Especially since it's via a legal deed, signed by her parents at the moment of her birth, stipulating that clones will be harvested for her and that, automatically, as soon as one of her organs breaks down, they will remove it from me, as they must have removed organs from my predecessors, and as they would from the fresh young Marie if I hadn't taken action.

Apparently the clone stock becomes weaker over time. So there's a sort of expiry date. A bit like yoghurt. You can make yoghurt with yoghurt for a fair while, and then, from time to time, all the same, you have to get hold of new yoghurt. If you see what I mean. If you've ever transferred yoghurt culture into a yoghurt-maker. They even came up with the idea of deep-freezing, but that was the end of us offshoots. Which is why there's now a limited lifespan for any of Frankenstein's monsters. (That's what some of us call the offshoots. Frankenstein's monster was a fictional creature. A creature made out of various body parts.)

A brain transplant is their cut-off point. They tried a thousand times with monkeys: it works, but it only extends the life of the brain, not the body. It's the brain's ego that survives, but the container, the face and all the rest of the body, is nothing more than a walking corpse. And even then, it seems the ego doesn't cope well with the brain transplant. It seems there are worse things than death.

Where was I?

I'm cold.

Oh yes. My clicker and I were watching that video. I asked him again if he could replay the sea. That supernatural, turquoise sea. I used to think the sea was always murky, black, terrifying. We have a book by Victor Hugo in the encampment (Victor Hugo was a nineteenth-century writer), in which I found this sentence: 'A strange sense of sombre expectation hung over the sea.' I say it over and over to myself. I don't know why, but this sentence makes me feel better. We can never listen to music here: the little battery power we have is reserved for more necessary functions. 'A strange sense of sombre expectation hung over the sea.' This sentence made it seem as if the sea was an immense reservoir of possibilities. Anyway. That was not at all the sea on the video. I couldn't stop asking the clicker to replay the images, again and again. A bit more and we could have been at the cinema. At the drive-in in the forest!

(Drive-ins were open-air cinemas; our ancestors used to drive there and watch films from their cars.) I wanted to keep looking at the old woman. The pureblood. The woman for whom I was born. The one for whom Marie and I, and perhaps others exactly like us, were born. I found the whole thing difficult to take on board. For weeks, I found it difficult. It seemed so hard to believe. It requires a radical change of thinking, really, to no longer see yourself at the centre of things—at the centre of your own vision of the world. To understand that you are nothing more than a peripheral offshoot. Required by people very far away, light years away from you. Who have decided, *bingo*, that you would be born, that you would be harvested, then taken to pieces. I felt like Copernicus (Copernicus was a scholar from I-can't-remember-which century), who worked out that the Sun doesn't orbit the Earth, but that the Earth orbits the Sun.

The Earth isn't at the centre. It's true. It's not at the centre of anything, as my clicker explained to me. We see the Milky Way as if it were a ribbon. We believe we're in the middle of the ribbon, at the crossroads of different pathways, if you like. Not at all. The ribbon is an optical illusion. The Milky Way is a large spiral, a disc, as are most galaxies. And we see the disc side-on. We're right on the edge, on the edge of the disc, not at all in the centre, but rather so lost out on the periphery that we see the spiral in cross-section.

We are small and spinning in the cosmos, and the life forms we've discovered elsewhere, people who probably look like us (well, anyway, we don't have a clue), are too far away for us ever to be able to talk to them.

So, there you go.

My clicker holds me tight. I'm out of breath. He's almost hurting me.

Apparently at my age, not that old, we don't have a single original cell. All our cells have automatically replaced themselves. All our body tissues renew themselves several times in the course of our lives. Our heart and our brain take longer, I think, but most of the organs in our bodies are routinely less than ten years old and are continuously regenerating. A red blood cell, for example, lives for only a very short time. Likewise for the cells in our eyes.

I'm cold.

I'm frightened that I'll get an infection in my one and only kidney. It's wearing out. Admittedly, they could always transplant one of Marie's kidneys; it wouldn't kill her to have only one kidney. But (if you've been following me) I have become completely opposed to this use of the halves. To this use of us.

I'm afraid the only truly durable bit of my body is the electrical box. The unit implanted in my grey matter. Fortunately, thanks to my skull, to my sturdy, hermetically sealed cranium, I can't feel it. I think I'd go crazy if I could feel it beneath my skin. Fortunately, I've got a Tupperware head, ha! Otherwise I couldn't help operating on myself, like I did with my dog, Wolf, and when I removed my implants, with one small, clean incision. The main thing is to perform it with conviction. No hesitation. You cut, and that's it. No soul-searching. Get a grip. I'd be up for it, if I could feel that thing moving under my fingers. If I could feel how hard it was, its corners. In the mush of my grey matter. It gives me electric shocks. Perhaps it's malfunctioning. It's emitting things I can't control anymore. It's not good. I no longer have any resistance. In the past, I felt as if I knew how to erect my own immune defence system against the things inside me. As if I knew how to detect them and stop them. But perhaps the problem is in my own brain—tissues becoming necrotic from contact with the unit—and not at all the unit itself that is corroding, as I'd hoped was the case. Or perhaps the corrosion is attacking my brain.

I'm a robot like the others.

I'm tired of it all.

I have to hurry.

They must all be out digging somewhere.

They say you have to turn the page. You often hear those words, even in the forest. In fact, some even want to drop the whole business. But before turning that page, I'd like us to read to the bottom of it. All of it, even the fine print, the footnotes and the appendices, everything. I'd like to be certain, if one day someone finds this notebook in the forest, buried in the tin, perhaps with my bones, I'd like to be certain that, before it's destroyed, or, I don't know, they say I made it all up, or they make fun of it, anyway, I'd like to be certain that it's read to the end. That's all.*

I have no idea how I'm managing to write. How

---

* And don't go thinking that I'm not certain I'm not a non-person.

I managed to get to this point.

Perhaps we're only digging to escape from any more organ removals, and not in order to save the world.

Sometimes I imagine myself in the tin. I see myself, in the tin, all squashed up, still alive, I have no idea how, still writing, all contorted and no longer even managing to read what I'm writing.

Safe place, my arse.

I remember our bodies used to function like computer mice. Perhaps I'm still moving my hand, my arm, a tiny bit and it's still writing, almost without me. Ha!

And if my bones are found with my writing, if I'm still here, mummified or whatever, with my skull empty and the electrical box lying at the bottom, durable and still beeping, still sending those damn electrical impulses into oblivion, in the tin, in the forest or what will be left of it, in the smoking debris of the burnt-out forest, the electrical box fallen into the hollow of my cranium and still issuing orders and imposing thoughts which, had they reached my consciousness distinctly, would have appalled me, I would like you, please, to read this as a prayer,

I would like you to consider my poor bones, my poor dry cellular tissues, to consider them with the tenderness that elephants reserve for their dead. Apparently, in the past, when there were elephants, wild elephants or almost wild, when you could still see elephants living in nature, apparently they would come to a stop in their slow and thoughtful walking. Apparently they stopped when they found bones of other elephants. They contemplated the long, empty ribs over the missing heart, the enormous skull over the lost thoughts, the long tusks (if they hadn't been poached), the spinal column that was as long and sturdy as a railway line. They stopped and, with their flexible trunks, they clasped the blanched bits of bone and lifted them up, and they held them gently, in the air they were breathing, for those who were no longer breathing. And they set off again, heavy and pensive, contemplating the world with their sad little eyes, for those who no longer saw it. If you find these bones in this tin, I would like you, please, to think for a few seconds about the woman who once breathed here.

I'm in the forest and I can no longer breathe. I can no longer see very well. I can no longer make sense of anything at all. I can no longer see the trees, because I'm probably being kept inside the tunnels. I'm cold.

It feels like I'm alone now.